FRIEND I

If ever Skye Fargo needed a friend, it was in the hellhole mining town called Central City, where killers were out to gun him down, and the law was set to string him up. Maybe that was why he was so glad to see Jessie Sawyer for the first time since a memorable night three years back.

But there were a couple of other reasons, too. As Jessie stripped her chemise over her head and smiled, Skye stepped back to take a good look at those reasons in all their beauty.

"You haven't changed a lick," Skye said.

"I hope you haven't," Jessie said, looking his powerful body up and down.

"Not in the ways that count," said Skye, smiling.

"Not that I don't believe you," said Jessie, as she wrapped her arms around his neck, "but you're going to have to prove it."

The Trailsman didn't mind. After all, what were friends for . . . ?

THE
WAYWARD
LASSIE

by

Jon Sharpe

A SIGNET BOOK

NEW AMERICAN LIBRARY

PUBLISHED BY
THE NEW AMERICAN LIBRARY
OF CANADA LIMITED

PUBLISHER'S NOTE

This novel is a work of fiction. Names, characters, places, and incidents either are the product of the author's imagination or are used fictitiously, and any resemblance to actual persons, living or dead, events, or locales is entirely coincidental.

NAL BOOKS ARE AVAILABLE AT QUANTITY DISCOUNTS
WHEN USED TO PROMOTE PRODUCTS OR SERVICES.
FOR INFORMATION PLEASE WRITE TO PREMIUM MARKETING DIVISION,
NEW AMERICAN LIBRARY, 1633 BROADWAY,
NEW YORK, NEW YORK 10019.

Copyright © 1986 by Jon Sharpe

First Printing, December, 1986

2 3 4 5 6 7 8 9

SIGNET TRADEMARK REG. U.S. PAT. OFF. AND FOREIGN COUNTRIES
REGISTERED TRADEMARK — MARCA REGISTRADA
HECHO EN WINNIPEG, CANADA

SIGNET, SIGNET CLASSIC, MENTOR, ONYX, PLUME, MERIDIAN
AND NAL BOOKS are published in Canada by The New American
Library of Canada, Limited, 81 Mack Avenue, Scarborough,
Ontario, Canada M1L 1M8
PRINTED IN CANADA
COVER PRINTED IN U.S.A.

The Trailsman

Beginnings . . . they bend the tree and they mark the man. Skye Fargo was born when he was eighteen. Terror was his midwife, vengeance his first cry. Killing spawned Skye Fargo, ruthless, cold-blooded murder. Out of the acrid smoke of gunpowder still hanging in the air, he rose, cried out a promise never forgotten.

The Trailsman, they began to call him all across the West: searcher, scout, hunter, the man who could see where others only looked, his skills for hire but not his soul, the man who lived each day to the fullest, yet trailed each tomorrow. Skye Fargo, the Trailsman, the seeker who could take the wildness of a land and the wanting of a woman and make them his own.

*1861, St. Louis, Missouri,
the end of one trail,
beginning of another*

1

Fargo came groaning out of deep, deep sleep. He was so thoroughly disoriented that he wasn't even aware of it.

His tongue felt like it had grown scales during the night, and his throat seemed coated with a green, nauseous slime. His eyes were glued closed. He forced them open, slowly, one at a time, and discovered dark-brown hair on the pillow next to him. He could remember nothing about the previous night, but he sure as hell must have had a good time. Must have.

Good time or no, though, the loss of an entire evening was worrisome. He simply wasn't the kind of glad-handing hale fellow who went out and got himself wiped-out drunk. He did not permit himself that sort of thing.

Except this time.

He groaned aloud and rolled onto his back. It was a mistake. The movement, slight though it had been, set off a pounding inside his head that would have done credit to a bass drum on the Fourth of July. Son of a bitch!

The movement also roused the woman who was sleeping beside him. She stirred and rubbed at her eyes, whimpering a little as she came out of her sleep, then turned her head. Her eyes—light brown flecked with gold, he saw now—sparkled into a smile that didn't reach her lips.

"Good morning, Skye." She sounded pleased. Perhaps even a bit smug. My, but he did wish he could remember the night's events.

Fargo blinked, yawned, took another look at her. She wasn't bad-looking. Nice-enough features except for a small scar at the corner of her mouth. The imperfection was certainly not enough to worry about.

She sat up, the sheet that covered the two of them falling to her waist as she raised her arms to fluff her hair. It was a deceptively casual but quite thoroughly contrived action that all women know shows off their breasts to best advantage. She had much to show off. More than a mouthful, and therefore something of a waste. But such a lovely waste. Her breasts were large, firm for their size, and pink-tipped.

In spite of the drumbeat inside his head and the vile taste in his mouth, Fargo found himself becoming aroused. Whatever might have happened during the night, it certainly didn't slow him down this morning.

It occurred to him that he had no earthly idea of who this woman was or what her name might be. That was easily covered. "Good morning, honey."

She gave him a huge smile and a squeal of pleasure when she saw the sheet over his waist begin to rise into a tentlike form. "You need a hair of the dog, Skye. But nothing serious, hmm? Can I get you a beer? Then we can snuggle back into bed for a little while. We don't have to get up so early, do we?"

"That sounds . . . sounds fine." His damned tongue was not only scaly, it refused to function properly.

"Be right back, Skye." She bent down to give him a brief but highly promising kiss on the mouth—Lordy, he wouldn't have been able to stand the thought of kissing a foul thing like his mouth was this morning; his breath surely must be bad enough to gag a goat—and slipped out of the bed. The rest of her body wasn't bad either. Her ass was nicely rounded if a bit flabby. She had a pimple on her left cheek. But Fargo could easily live with that if she could.

She paused at the door to blow him another kiss, pulled on a light wrapper, and went into the hallway.

In addition to having no idea of who his sleeping companion was, Fargo couldn't remember where in the hell he was. The fact that she'd gone out in that skimpy robe hinted that they were not in a hotel. A whorehouse? Private home? He just didn't know.

About all he knew—and he wouldn't claim to be a hundred percent positive about that either—was that he was in St. Louis. He'd been paid off here—assuming he really was still in St. Louis and hadn't somehow misplaced a thousand miles or so of countryside—after escorting a small but valuable cargo of gemstones from Santa Fe east to the queen city of the West. And now, by damn, he had a hefty poke in his jeans pocket. Enough money that he could take some time for himself and do some serious searching for those sons of bitches who . . . He shook his head impatiently. No point in thinking about that right now. It just got him upset, thinking about the quest that drove him after the men he so desperately wanted—needed—to find and to kill.

He heard footsteps in the hall. The door opened, and the woman was back. She carried a small tin bucket in one hand and a pair of tin mugs in the other. She smiled at him again.

"That didn't take long."

"Of course not." Still no clues about where they were. Or who she was. He wished he could remember more. More? Hell, he wished he could remember anything.

The woman set the mugs on a bureau and poured foamy beer into them, handing the first to Fargo and taking a smaller portion for herself. "This will make you feel better, Skye."

It did. The sharp flavor cut through the fur on his teeth, washed most of the slime out of his throat, and even seemed to make some of the pounding in his head go away. Some, not all. He still felt like a sack of soggy shit. He was almost used to it, though.

The woman looked at him and smiled, barely tasting her drink. She set her mug aside and took his from his hand to put it out of the way also. With a broad smile she let the wrapper fall off her shoulders and slid under the sheet beside him.

Her mouth covered his hungrily and her hand searched for him, impatiently shoving the sheet aside and groping until she found him.

Fargo responded with an animal intensity. He moved, taking her right nipple in his mouth and pulled on it with a sudden hunger. He pulled on it again, harder this time, and the woman's mouth opened in a breathless moan of pleasure.

She clutched at him, grasping him, running her hand up and down the length of him, cupping his balls and applying pressure that stopped just short of becoming pain. Her breath was coming quicker. And so was his.

"You're special, Skye. So special." She lay flat on the bed, pulling him over her, and he moved from her breast, down across the soft mound of her belly to tangle in the curling patch of hair at her crotch.

She groaned and parted her thighs, opening herself to his touch. He dipped a finger into her to moisten the tip, then sought and rubbed the tiny button of woman-pleasure that was hidden in the pink folds of flesh there. He rubbed it slowly, in small circles, and she responded within moments, raising her hips to meet his touch, moaning and sighing, her own arousal evident with the quickening tempo of her responses until with a sharp, unexpected cry she clenched her legs tight together and stiffened in a spasm of raw pleasure.

Fargo kissed her gently, allowing her time to come down from the heights she had just reached.

Within seconds she was responding to the kiss, wrapping her arms around him and guiding him over her eager body, guiding him inside.

The heat of her surrounded and enveloped him, and he plunged deep into her. She kept her hand between their bodies, moving it lower to cup its heat around his balls even when he was inside her. The combined sensations of palm and woman-flesh worked together to bring him to a fast, thunderous climax.

He groaned as the spurting jets of hot fluid poured from his body deep into hers, and she held him all the tighter as he stiffened and shuddered and expended himself totally inside her.

When he was done, he collapsed, dropping his weight onto her sweaty, willing body, and she wrapped both arms tightly around him with a sigh of contentment. She seemed every bit as satisfied as he felt himself at the moment. It was quite a step up after the way he'd felt when he woke.

"Mmmm." He rooted for a moment in the hollow of her throat, relaxing, then rolled away from her.

"Can I get you anything else, Skye?"

"After that? I can't think of anything that would top it. But if you can, honey, I'm willing to listen to suggestions."

She laughed and sat up on the side of the bed to get the beers she had poured earlier. She handed Fargo his, and he took another satisfying swallow. Damn, but he wished he could remember more about her. She was something special. Certainly not a bad treat to wake up to on a bleary morning.

If it was still morning. The sunshine beyond her curtained window was strong enough to suggest that he might already have missed the morning and be working on the afternoon hours now.

There was quite a bit he wished he could remember.

He stood, wobbling only a little from the aftereffects of the night before, and reached for his clothes, dropped in an untidy pile on his side of the bed.

"You aren't leaving, are you Skye?" She sounded disappointed.

"Got to." He had plans. Plans that did not involve the soft living of St. Louis. Pleasant living, true, but not what he had in mind for the next few months. He had more than enough money now to finance the search for the men who had turned him from a normal young man into the avenger he had become.

"You'll see me again?"

"Sure, honey."

"You won't forget?"

"Forget you? Impossible." He finished buttoning his shirt and leaned down to give her a reassuring kiss. Damn, but he wished he knew who she was. He really might want to pay her another visit if he had time before he left.

He buckled his gun belt into place, automatically checking the Army Colt .44 to see that it was in good shape and that the brassy gleam of fresh caps showed on the steel nipples. The Sharps carbine leaned against the wall in a corner beside the door.

Best of all was the comforting weight of the gold pulling at his trousers and making a large lump in his pocket. Whoever the woman was, she was no sneak thief. Good. He needed that money to carry him on his search. His efforts on behalf of another man had paid off handsomely enough that Skye Fargo, the Trailsman, could conduct some business of his own.

"I'll see you later, honey," he said.

"See that you do, Skye. I miss you already. I want

more of that." On those last few words her voice dropped into a husky sultriness and her eyes quite deliberately strayed below his belt buckle.

Fargo smiled and let himself out into the hallway.

The staircase led down into a kitchen, large and commercial, and then out into a saloon, nearly empty at this time of day, whatever that was. A large clock over the bar indicated it was nearly 2 P.M. Fargo couldn't remember sleeping that late in . . . Hell, he couldn't remember ever sleeping that late. Period. He must really have had some time last night.

He went out onto the street—he was still in St. Louis—and the strong sunlight hit his eyes like a blow.

The thought of food no longer seemed so repulsive as it would have earlier. There was a café down the street, and he headed for that, feeling his pocket to satisfy himself that he had enough small change to pay for a meal. Although at this hour it probably would be impossible to get breakfast. He would have to settle for lunch.

He found no small coins so would have to dip into the gold Señor Martínez had paid him from the Santa Fe trip. No problem. He pulled out his pouch and opened it.

And spilled a pile of lead slugs into his palm.

2

Fargo whirled and raced back through the saloon, taking the back staircase three steps at a time. He burst into the room with the Colt in his fist and a cold glitter in his lake-blue eyes.

He was too late. The woman was gone.

For a moment he thought he might have the wrong room. But no, the bed was there, rumpled and sweaty as he remembered it. And the tin bucket containing the dregs of the beer they had shared, both mugs set tidily beside it now.

"Jesus!" Fargo blurted.

Frustration and fury churned inside his queasy gut. Fury because of his loss. He had been counting on that money. He needed it. Fury, too, because he had been duped by the damned woman. The bitch! She'd been so cool about the whole thing. She could have taken his money and left during the night. But no, she had remained right there, sleeping beside him, waking to take him into her arms and use the man she had so deliberately betrayed. Jezebel was what she was.

The frustration of it was almost worse than the fury.

Frustration because, now that she was gone, there was no one to strike back at in exchange for the betrayal.

"Bitch," he accused out loud to the empty room. It didn't make him feel any better. He hadn't expected it to.

He turned and went back downstairs, much more slowly than he had come up. The bartender and few midafternoon customers looked at him curiously. He had gone through in a hell of a hurry and with the Colt in his hand. Now at least he was a little calmer.

"The woman," Fargo asked, "where is she?"

"What woman?" The barman sounded bored and not in the slightest worried.

"The one that was upstairs with me last night."

The bartender shrugged. "Mister, I don't know nothing about any woman or about what you done last night. First place, I only work days. Second place, I don't ask no questions."

"Is this a saloon or some kind of half-assed hotel? I spent the night upstairs in one of those rooms, with a woman I don't even know. How the hell did I get there?"

The barman shrugged again. "I wouldn't know about that, mister. Sometimes customers use the spare rooms. As a favor, you know. Guy gets horny an' can't wait. Or passes out drunk an' nobody knows where to cart the body. Like that. Me, I wouldn't know. Like I said, I only work days." The man turned away from the unwanted line of inquiry and began needlessly polishing glasses.

A customer several paces away looked at Fargo and snickered. Questions like Fargo's were undoubtedly amusing to some son of a bitch who wasn't out a wallet of gold.

Thoroughly enraged but unwilling to take it out on ignorant strangers, Fargo turned and stalked out before he bought himself more trouble. Trouble he had enough of already, thank you.

He got out onto the street and turned toward the café.

Then it occurred to him that he was dead, flat, starkers busted.

He couldn't even afford to buy himself a meal.

How he was going to pay the Ovaro out of hock at the damned livery he wouldn't even think about right now.

Jesus!

So instead of eating, he headed for the nearest patch of shade and hunkered in it to try to get a handle on things.

He was broke. If he had a home, he would have been far away from it.

Home. That was the thing, wasn't it? Skye Fargo had had a home once. Long ago and far away. He'd also had a different name then. Until that night those sons of bitches came and murdered his entire family. Until the night the man who was now known as the Trailsman vowed to find and punish them for destroying everything and everyone he held dear. And that search had been what his heavy poke was intended for. He had expected to use that money to free himself from the necessity of work and concentrate solely on the trail that had begun in his own personal, private hell.

Well, that was out. Now he was going to have to find something, and damned soon, just to eat on and pay the livery.

"Shit." He muttered and mumbled to himself some, but that solved nothing.

He said it again anyway. "Shit."

He wondered if that man—what the hell had his name been, anyway?—was still needing someone.

Flush with the profits of the trip over from Santa Fe, Fargo had scarcely paid any attention when the man approached him a couple days earlier and asked him to take on a job. Fargo hadn't even asked what the job was, just brushed the fellow off and went on with his plans for the future.

Now the prospect of a job—any job—would be almighty interesting.

He tried to think. Conley? Conway? Something like that. Conroy. That was it. Or was it? He couldn't be sure. He'd recognize the fellow, though. He was sure of that.

Conroy, if that was his name, had approached him down at the livery when he was there checking to make sure that the Ovaro was properly stalled and bedded and comfortable. But now, if Fargo wanted to find this Conroy fellow he was going to have to make a search of St. Louis. The prospect wasn't thrilling.

Fargo stood and began to amble through the saloon districts, pausing at every door to peer inside. This could turn out to be a long, slow, and hungry chore.

While he walked, he thought, trying to remember what could have happened last night.

It wasn't like him to allow himself to get that drunk. The years of razor-edge danger had put a razor's edge on his self-control and on his caution. He just didn't do things like that. Yet apparently he had.

He found a public trough and pump, worked the handle to start a stream of fresh, cold water out of the spout, and stuck his head under it, soaking the thick ruff of lank black hair that curled down over his forehead and at the back of his dark-tanned neck. He felt a little better after that, better still after he swallowed near a quart of the icy water.

Funny, but the water set as easy on his stomach as the beer had earlier when the woman brought it for him. It had been a long time since he had permitted himself the careless luxury of a drunken spree, but the way he remembered it, a load of water should threaten to bring back the inebriation.

He felt nothing like that now.

He walked in the sunshine and thought some more.

Bits and pieces were coming back to him now.

Nothing at all about the woman. Not a glimmer of memory about her.

But he seemed to recall that he saw to the Ovaro's comforts and got to chatting with some drifter there at the livery. A quiet, forgettable sort of fellow. And something about an invitation to have a beer. At the saloon where he had awakened? He couldn't be sure. Possibly. One beer.

He and the drifter who'd been talking with him had had—he tried to get it clear in his thoughts—they'd had just that one beer together.

And it hadn't been in any saloon. They'd sat on a public bench. Under a big tree. An elm, he thought. The memories were coming clearer to him now. Once started, they flowed the way they should have to begin with.

Yes, dammit. There was that drifter. Talk about the country to the west of St. Louis. Talk about the Rockies, way the hell and gone to the west. That invitation. Wandering along, still talking, until they sat down on that bench. And the drifter'd said something about fetching them both a beer. He'd gone off someplace and come back with two of them.

But there had been nothing stronger than beer, dammit, and only the one of those.

On an impulse Fargo turned back the way he had come, his stride lengthening with impatience until he reached the block with the saloon where he had awakened this morning.

The elm tree was there, in that block, on the opposite side of the street. The public bench was there, just as he remembered it now.

So he'd been set up. And damned nicely too. A casual encounter. A casual offer. One lousy beer drunk on a public street.

Someone must have put something into the beer. A mickey. Whatever it was, it had worked entirely too well. Put him out as cold as a stone and let him wake up befuddled and confused. With the damned woman there beside him to confuse things all the more.

"Shit," he told the world at large again.

There was no mystery about the motive the bitch and her pal had had: it was that pouch of Mexican gold coins in his pocket. That was what they'd wanted, and they had damn sure gotten it.

Understanding didn't solve Fargo's current problems. But it was a start.

Right now he needed to find Conroy and see if he couldn't get a fresh start on things.

And in the meantime, if he ran into that bitch or her drifter friend, well, Skye Fargo would just have to have a word with them. Or two.

He felt a little better now. Certainly more purposeful. This time, when he started making his rounds through the tenderloin district of St. Louis, he was looking for any of three people, not just for one.

And of the three of them, the one he would most like to see was the woman.

"Mr. Fargo." The man sounded surprised and pleased to see him.

Fargo in his turn was pretending also that it was a chance encounter. He didn't want Conroy to know that the Trailsman had been seeking him for the past several days.

Several damned hungry days, as a matter of fact. The only thing he had had to eat during that time was a little early fruit he had been able to plunder from unattended orchards and a few vegetables taken from garden plots here and there.

"Yes. Mr. Conroy, isn't it?"

"Fitzroy," the man corrected.

No wonder Fargo's inquiries had met no success. He'd forgotten the name.

"Are you still intent on your own business, Fargo?"

"As a matter of fact"—the Trailsman helped himself to a chair at Fitzroy's table—"I'd consider a job now. If you still need my kind of help."

"Gracious, yes. Can I buy you a drink?"

"I'd like that," Fargo admitted. And not only because he could use a beer about now. More important, there was a mouth-wateringly tempting free lunch spread out at the end of the bar.

Fitzroy motioned for a waiter to come and Fargo went to the free-lunch spread and heaped a plate high with slices of ham and pickled eggs. The beer had been delivered to Fitzroy's table by the time he returned.

"Tell me more about what it is you're needing," Fargo invited around a mouthful of ham and crackers.

"I'm a wealthy man," Fitzroy said by way of preamble, "but I'm growing no younger." Fargo would have guessed him to be in his fifties or possibly even later. "The older I become, Fargo, the more aware I am of regrets. Can a young, vigorous man such as yourself understand that?"

"I think so."

"Perhaps. Perhaps not. Most your age and many a great deal older tend to think that money is important, Mr. Fargo. Let me tell you, sir, that it is not." Fitzroy sighed and looked off in thought for a moment. Then he shook himself, returning to the here and now, and continued. "I have money, Mr. Fargo, but I am beginning to learn that there are things of much greater importance. Friends. Decency. Most of all, family." He said that last with a trace of sorrow in his voice.

"Family," the Trailsman repeated. "Yes, Mr. Fitzroy. I can understand the importance of family."

Fitzroy would have no way to know it, but the man had struck a strong chord of sympathy in Skye Fargo when he spoke of family and their importance. Particularly when

22

their loss was a void that could never be filled this side of the grave.

"It is not important that you know the entire story of my past, Mr. Fargo. Suffice it to say, sir, that I was once young and very foolish, as I suspect many young men are. I placed my values on material things. Acquisitions. On things of only fleeting value." Fitzroy sighed again and reached for his glass of beer.

"I had a family then," he said sadly. "I didn't value them. Not by half enough. My . . . my wife was perhaps more sensible than I. She left me. I don't blame her. She had more than enough cause. And I am afraid it is far too late for me to—how shall I put this?—to rectify my errors."

Fargo raised an eyebrow.

"My wife . . . she remarried, so I suppose I shouldn't call her that any longer, but it is still the way I think of her, as a good and true wife much better than I deserved or at the time wanted. My wife is dead now. I established that fact some time ago. As I said, too late. There is no way I can ever show that good woman that I was wrong, that I realize my error and want to make up for it. But we had a child, my wife and I. I . . . I hate to admit this to a stranger, but you are entitled to know. I as much as abandoned the both of them. And more the shame to me for it, but it is the simple truth, sir. I abandoned my wife and my child and sought my fortune. Now I have the fortune, but it is the child that I miss." Fitzroy had to stop speaking for a moment while he put his emotions back in order.

"You have a reputation, Mr. Fargo. I've done considerable asking, looking for someone who might be able to help me. Indeed, I've hired several private-detective firms in the East. Their fees were large but their results unimpressive. I won't claim that you are my last hope, Mr. Fargo. No matter what your answer to me, I shan't quit my search. But what I would like, what I would beseech of you, sir, is your help in finding my little girl. I would pay well for your services. My hope, sir, is that the man who is called the Trailsman can find the trail of my missing child and bring her back to me after my years of regret.''

''What makes you think I could find her when your private detectives couldn't?''

''They could not locate her, Mr. Fargo, but they believe she may have come west to the little-populated territories. West of civilization, as they say. And what I hear is that no man is as knowledgeable as you are when it comes to the wild places.''

''Would she still have your name?''

Fitzroy shook his head. ''Probably not, although that is only a guess. She likely would have been located by now if that were so.''

''Any reason why she'd change it? Or any idea what she could've changed it to? Like a stepfather's name, something like that?''

''I have searched for her under my name and her stepfather's, of course, but to no avail. As for what else she might have changed it to, I couldn't say. Perhaps she married.''

''I thought she was a child,'' Fargo said.

''Gracious. I'm terribly sorry. It has been many years since my wife and I parted. Margaret Anne would be twenty-four now. I have a picture of her, if that would help.'' He reached into an inside coat pocket and pulled out a tattered, age-wrinkled folder of pasteboard. He opened it and handed it across to Fargo.

It was a very old daguerreotype, as faded and wrinkled as the folder Fitzroy kept it in, that showed a child of no more than four or five, seated in an artificially rigid pose, dressed in what had obviously been her very best. Her hair was curly, her face plump. Little more than that could be made out from the picture.

"I know," Fitzroy said sadly. "It can't help very much. But it is all of her that I have. She had . . . has . . . red hair. Might that help?"

Fargo shrugged. The man was giving him damned little to go on.

"I will pay you, Mr. Fargo. Whatever you ask. And a bonus—name your amount—if you can locate her for me. Margaret Anne is all the hope that I have in this world, Mr. Fargo. And after my past . . . perhaps all the hope that I shall ever have."

"You'd have to level with me, Fitzroy. Everything you can remember. Names. Places your, uh, wife might have been. Anything you know about her or the child. Everything."

The Trailsman had not yet committed himself to this trial. Not in so many words, anyway. But in truth, there was no way he could not take on this job now that he knew what it was. Fitzroy wanted to be reunited with a family he had once abandoned. Skye Fargo would have given his very soul for one minute of reunion with the family that had been stolen from him.

There was no way he could refuse to help a man whose hope was the very one Fargo would have given anything to attain for himself.

"Anything, Mr. Fargo. Anything at all," Fitzroy said with feeling.

"Then I'll do for you whatever I can, Mr. Fitzroy. So long as you understand I can make you no promises. Except to give you the very best that I can. That I can promise."

Fitzroy smiled for the first time since he had begun talking. He extended his hand across the table and Skye Fargo shook it.

*　　*　　*

The private-detective's report—Fitzroy showed it to him, penned in a precise, careful hand and then signed in an indecipherable scrawl—indicated that Martha Simmons Fitzroy married Donald Powell, Jr., on February 18, 1849, in Cincinnati, Ohio. Powell was listed on tax rolls there for the next decade. The investigation showed that Powell was a surveyor by training and an engineer by self-declaration. In 1859, exact date unknown, the Powells left Ohio and moved west to Virginia City, Montana Territory. Martha Powell died there June 4, 1860. By that time Fitzroy had been looking for her, and for their daughter, for nearly half a year.

He had come close, Fargo thought. But no cigar.

The current whereabouts, name, marital status of Margaret Anne were unknown.

Judging from what Fitzroy said he had paid for the private-investigation firm to look for his missing family, the man had not gotten a hell of a lot. Still, if he felt any resentment, he didn't show it in the slightest. Apparently he really was willing to pay any amount to find his daughter. Certainly he hadn't balked about giving Skye Fargo an advance that was several times more than Fargo would have had nerve enough to ask for. And there was still the promise of a substantial bonus if or when the girl was found.

"You don't know anything more than this about her?" Fargo had asked.

"No. Nothing, I'm sorry to say."

"And you haven't been to Virginia City yourself to make inquiries?"

"No. I would have gone, of course, although I've heard it can be an uncivilized sort of place. I got the impression there was something . . . I don't know what, but possibly some kind of trouble. In any event, the investigator I hired wanted to be relieved from the search. I would have gone to Virginia City myself then, except that I heard about you. And that you were actually right here in St. Louis. So I contacted you instead.''

"All right, then," Fargo had told him. Fitzroy had given Fargo an address in New York City where Fargo could reach him by telegraph if he had anything to report. Or if Fargo needed more money to conduct his hunt.

"Anything," Fitzroy had said. "Anything at all that you need. I'll gladly supply it." Fargo had believed him. He had seen the intensity in Fitzroy's eyes.

It was something Skye Fargo understood. Very much the same sort of look he himself might have had if there had been any faint hope that he might someday again see his own murdered loved ones.

Fargo had more sense than to admit it to Fitzroy, but he would have worked on this one for the man for twenty-five cents a day. This opportunity to reunite one lost family was something that was quickly taking on a personal meaning for the Trailsman that went beyond a mere job and approached being a quest.

Virginia City, though, was one hell of a distance from St. Louis.

Still, there was no necessity for speed here. It had been nineteen years since Fitzroy had seen Margaret Anne. Days wouldn't exactly matter now. It was the long run that was important.

There were basically two routes Fargo could have chosen to reach Virginia City and the start of his search. Overland, via the old Oregon Trail and then up the Bozeman Cutoff. Or by water, on a steamer as far as the undependable water levels would permit and then by road or trail from there. Since he was already virtually on the riverfront at St. Louis, with steamers docking almost daily and traffic flowing out of the city like spokes from a hub,

Fargo decided to make the first portion of the trip in comfort.

Fitzroy's money bought the stout Ovaro pinto out of the livery and bought passage for man and horse alike on the side-wheel steamer *Nellie Nye*.

"You could save yourself a seventy-dollar shippin' charge, son, by leavin' the horse here. Likely you don't know that western country good as I do," a well-intentioned riverman told him, "but there's horses cheap all through that country. Horse like that one, hell, son, you could sell 'im here in St. Louie for a hundred dollars, more or less, an' buy you a horse just as good at the upriver end for twenty. I swear it's so."

The riverman might know steam and water—the Trailsman had no way to judge that—but the man didn't know either Skye Fargo or the big pinto that had carried him through so much.

"I thank you for the advice, neighbor, but I'll pay the passage and take my horse along, thank you."

"But—"

For the first time Fargo's eyelids tightened and his lips were drawn back into an uncompromising firm set. "I said I thanked you for the advice. That I do. But I'm entitled to be all the damn fool I want, long as I pay for the privilege. Which I'm trying to do. Now, will you take my money and arrange the passage . . . for me *and* the horse? Or do I take my business elsewhere?"

"Whatever you say, mister. Whatever you say," the riverman said quickly. It had been "son" before; now it was "mister." And there was no more argument or instruction on the subject of what Skye Fargo was or wasn't permitted to take along with him on the side-wheeler.

The *Nellie Nye* was no gracious, floating palace of the Mississippi River trade. She was a Missouri River mongrel, basically a flat-bottomed, shallow draft barge with a steam engine plunked down in the center of things and a small paddle wheel set on either side. It was as ugly as it was awkward. But it would float in waters that would have ripped the bottom out of any "real" boat. Its claim was efficiency, not elegance.

A cabin of sorts had been erected amidships, a shack thrown up around the engine and used also for storage and kitchen purposes. An awning had been extended over the foredeck, where passengers could spend their leisure time lounging on the bales and boxes of cargo and where they could select deck space for their beds at night. Livestock pens had been constructed on the afterdeck. Except for Fargo's superb Ovaro, the aft passengers consisted mostly of crates of chickens and a few dairy goats. Human passengers were welcome to make their beds aft under the stars if they so chose.

The accommodations, all in all, would have to be classed as spartan. The *Nellie Nye* did, however, wallow steadily upriver in her slow, dependable, chuffing way.

Skye Fargo had no complaints. He had endured conditions that would have made this seem the lap of luxury, so for the moment he was content. That claim couldn't be said of all the passengers.

"Beans and corn bread. Beans and corn bread. Is this the only kind o' slop that nigger can make?" The speaker was a florid, balding man, very broad in face and body, who gave the impression of being soft, even fat, although Fargo noticed that there seemed to be little if any fat actually on him. He was built wide and bulky, but he moved with athletic quickness. His conversations with fellow passengers left no doubt that his sympathies lay with the southern states in the political fuss that was developing in the east.

Fargo scowled and opened his mouth to speak. The

cook was an unfailingly cheerful man who seemed to be doing his level best to make the passengers as comfortable as possible under the crude conditions of their travel. The fact that the cook was a freeman of color didn't alter any of that, and Fargo didn't think he deserved such casual treatment, particularly since he was standing right there when the remark was made. He couldn't have helped but hear, although he said nothing. Fargo was more than willing to comment on his behalf. But another passenger spoke up first.

"We'll not be having any more of that kind of talk, sir," the passenger said. "A man deserves to be judged by his actions, not his color. High time your kind learned that. And that you are subject to such judgment as much as any other."

The burly, florid fellow, whose name was Simms, gave the protesting passenger a look of disgust. "Another of those damned John Brown abolitionists." He fairly spat the name at the protester, who was a much smaller and most inoffensive-looking man.

"John Brown's dead, more's the pity, but I'd not be shamed to be found in that company."

"Huh! Murderers and thieves in that company of his. Bunch of nigger-lovers." Simms glared first toward the cook, who hadn't said a word during any of this, and then at his fellow passengers.

"Let's not—" Fargo started to say, wanting to pour oil onto these troubled waters. But again he was too late.

The small man, who as far as Fargo knew had never given his name, stood. The Trailsman believed then and later that the fellow's intent was no more harmful or serious than to walk away and end the course this conversation was taking.

Simms, though, either misunderstood or pretended to.

Without warning, Simms threw his plate of beans and excellent corn bread into the smaller man's face.

Simms followed through with deadly quick intent. His left arm swept out, clubbing the still-silent cook aside as he leapt on his much smaller opponent.

The northerner raised a hand as if to defend himself from the unprovoked assault, and again Simms chose to interpret the motion his own way.

Instead of starting a fistfight, which Simms would handily have won anyway, the southerner pulled a knife and rammed it deep into the little man's belly.

Fargo was a split second too late to turn the blow. He jumped forward as soon as he saw the flash of Simms's blade, but Simms struck before Fargo could cross the distance between them.

Fargo grabbed Simms' wrist and twisted, taking the knife away from the inexplicably irate southerner and tossing it overboard.

By then, though, it was already too late. The little man went pale. He clutched his hands over his stomach, but the gesture wasn't enough to hold back the flow of bright blood that was already staining the front of his shirt and seeping through the heavier material of his vest.

Simms tried to backhand the Trailsman.

That was a mistake.

Fargo ducked under the blow and stepped forward, under Simms' guard. He leaned into the blocky man and began to pound hard lefts and rights into Simms' belly.

Hitting Simms in the stomach was much like punching a clapboard wall.

Simms tried to knee Fargo in the crotch.

Fargo turned the knee aside with his thigh and gave Simms a tight, wicked grin that held no humor in it at all.

Simms tried again to kick Fargo in the groin. He gave it

his best shot. He might as well have. The damage had already been done.

Fargo avoided the kick with almost casual disdain. He skipped lightly to the side, hesitated for a fraction of a second until Simms was off balance, then lunged forward.

Fargo's right fist shot forward like a shell from a four-pounder, knuckles extended, his expression grim.

The blow caught Simms in the fragile cartilage of the throat, collapsing it instantly.

Simms gagged and grabbed for his neck, totally forgetting the Trailsman for that moment.

The moment was all Skye Fargo needed. He shifted his weight to his left foot and with the right planted the toe of his boot hard and fast into Simms' balls.

"Like I said, Mr. Simms. Your rules. My game."

Simms doubled forward, still grasping his neck with both hands, and Fargo kicked him flush in the face, snapping him upright again. Down and back up as quickly as a child's bottom-weighted punching toy.

Simms turned and staggered away from the furious onslaught of the Trailsman, blinded by pain and sudden fear. Either he didn't see the low gunwale or was so fearful of Fargo that he didn't care. He took four tottering steps forward, hit the thigh-high rail, and toppled over it into the dark, swirling waters of the Missouri.

The cook, who had not yet said a word throughout the encounter, walked to the gunwale and peered over the side.

"Man overboard," he said in a soft and rather pleased-sounding voice. But when he looked toward Fargo, his face was expressionless.

No other member of the crew could possibly have heard.

By then Fargo was no longer interested in Simms or what might become of him. If the son of a bitch lived, that was his good fortune. His tough luck if he didn't. Fargo was bending over the small man, who was slumped on the deck against a bale of woolen trade blankets.

The knife wound was little more than an elongated dimple on the flesh of the little man's stomach. At least so it appeared on the outside. There was no way to tell what damage had been done inside. The knife had been a hafted belt model with a blade probably five or six inches long. Fargo was almost sure it had gone into the man to the hilt. If so, the damage was probably extensive. Probably mortal.

"Son of a bitch," the little man said.

There were only two other passengers on the *Nellie Nye*. Both of them seemed intent on the serious business of looking elsewhere.

"The fight's over," Fargo said. "Safe for you to give me a hand now."

One of the men coughed once and cleared his throat loudly. At least he had the good grace to look ashamed. After a moment he set his plate aside and joined Fargo kneeling beside the wounded man. The other passenger continued to pretend that he had seen and heard nothing.

"Help me lift him up. We'll lay him over there. On top of those crates."

The cook helped, breaking open one of the bales of burlap-covered blankets and preparing a rude bed of sorts. Fargo and the other passenger lifted the man—he weighed next to nothing—as gently as they could and placed him onto the bed. Even though they were as careful as they could be, the man had to bite his underlip until he drew blood in order to shut off the scream of agony that tried to get past his lips.

"It's all right to holler," Fargo said gently. "We understand."

The little fellow shook his head stubbornly and held himself stiff and unyielding against the pain. Cold sweat beaded his forehead, standing out plain against the pale, clammy skin.

The passenger who had so reluctantly helped took another look at the wound and turned away. He looked like he was going to be sick. A moment later he was, leaning over the rail and retching, the sound of it mercifully lost in the slap of the paddles against the water and the constant drone of the engine turning.

"Am I dying?" the little man asked Fargo.

"I'm no doctor," Fargo evaded.

"Didn't ask you that. Tell me the truth. I have reason for asking." The man might be small, but he was not without bravery. And he sounded in full control of his faculties, not in the least bit panicked.

"I could be wrong," Fargo emphasized. "But if I had to guess, man, I'd say that you won't last to the next landing, where we might find a doctor."

The little man nodded as if it was the answer he fully expected.

"Do me . . ." He had to wait a moment while he clenched his teeth against a rush of pain. "Do me a favor? Please?"

"If I can."

"Inside coat pocket. Get it out for me."

Fargo held the lapel back and found the pocket. "There's nothing here," he said.

"Deeper. Down at . . . bottom."

Fargo reached inside again. He found it this time, a tiny packet wrapped in oilskin and tightly sewn. "This?"

The little man nodded. "Got to . . ." He stiffened and cried out. Then shook his head impatiently. "Got to get that . . . to Bozeman. Deliver it. Contact . . . Raye. Deliver. To Raye. Must . . . get it . . . to Raye. Help. Please."

"To Ray in Bozeman? Ray who? How do I find him?"

But it was already too late. Fargo was asking questions of a dead man.

Fargo stepped aside, and the cook, who may or may not have heard any of that, brought another blanket from the opened bale to stretch over the little man's still face.

Who or what the man had been, Fargo had no way to know. He shoved the oilskin packet into his pocket.

3

It was past dark when the tired black-and-white pinto carried an equally road-weary Skye Fargo into Bozeman. The ride had been longer than he expected. The water level in the upper Missouri was lower than had been reported downriver at St. Louis, and the *Nellie Nye* couldn't navigate beyond the Yellowstone. Fargo had hoped to stay with the Missouri all the way to the Musselshell.

The late arrival was no problem, though. Bozeman was open day or night to whatever pursuits a man might require. Fargo found a livery and wagon park not far off the well-lighted business district and dismounted to lead the Ovaro through a maze of empty wagons and mule-filled pens to find the hostler.

"One horse?" the man asked. He made it sound like there was something unusual about a traveler arriving unaccompanied. And perhaps there was at this northern terminus for the overland commerce from the States into Montana Territory.

"Just the one," Fargo told him.

The hostler looked the pinto over with a judicious eye and gained Fargo's approval when he said, "Just the one, but a good 'um. This big fella deserves special care."

"At a special cost?" Fargo asked skeptically.

The hostler snorted. "I know what you're thinking, but the price is the same for all. It's just that I don't get a chance much to see horses o' such quality. Be a pleasure takin' care o' him. Rate's a quarter a day. That's feedin' with hay only. Grain is ten cent a gallon extra." He raised an eyebrow in Fargo's direction.

"I'll have the grain for him too. Gallon a feeding, starting tomorrow morning. None tonight. Hay only to-night, and the water after."

The hostler grunted. Fargo took that for agreement.

"I'll be needing a place to stay for myself too," Fargo said. "And you might help me with something else. I'm looking for a man named Ray."

"Ray what?" The hostler took the reins from Fargo and with deft, sure motions stripped the bridle from the big Ovaro and replaced it with a halter. He put the pinto in a set of cross ties and began grooming the horse with slow, patient care. There was no need for Fargo to be concerned about the horse's treatment here. The man knew what he was doing.

"I don't know," Fargo admitted. "Just Ray."

The hostler paused to strip some loose hairs off the surface of the dandybrush and took the opportunity to give Fargo a searching look. "You don't look like a man in search of trouble."

"I'm not," Fargo assured him.

"Then you might wanta go easy when you ask questions about people name of Ray."

It was Fargo's turn to lift an eyebrow in unspoken question.

The hostler went back to his brushing. "Lots of fellas in town called Ray, I'd say," he said into the gleaming flank of the horse.

"But you do have a particular one in mind." It wasn't a question.

"Ayuh. 'Course it might not be the one *you* have in mind."

"That's a question I can't answer," Fargo said. "Like I told you, the first name is all I was given."

The hostler grunted again and worked on the pinto's coat without speaking for a while. He rubbed down the horse's legs and picked up the near fore. "Looks like you could stand for 'im to be trimmed and these shoes reset. Not critical yet, but it won't be long. Want me to do it for you?"

"If you wouldn't mind." There were not many strangers that he would allow to touch the Ovaro's feet, but he suspected that this was one who could do the job better than Fargo could himself.

"There's a man name of Ray Stone," the hostler went on as if there had been no interruption in the topic.

"But?"

The hostler went back to working on the pinto, apparently pondering whether he should say more or not. "But there's talk about Ray Stone," the man finally admitted.

"Talk?"

"Talk that it might not be a good idea to be seen too much in Stone's company. If you know what I mean."

"I just now rode into town. I guess I don't know what you mean."

"You know what a vigilance committee is, young fella?"

"Yes."

" 'Nuff said, then. You be careful you don't get tied in too close with Stone. Or I might be sorta inheriting this here fine animal by default."

"Thanks for the advice."

"No advice. Just an old man's idle chatter."

"Sure. But thanks anyway." Fargo picked up his saddle

and dumped it in a corner, unstrapped the saddlebags and bedroll, and threw them over his shoulder. He let the Sharps dangle from his left hand so it wouldn't seem a threat to anyone he passed on the street. Apparently Bozeman was in a nervous frame of mind.

Finding a hotel room was no problem. The town was well accustomed to visitors. Fargo deposited his gear and treated himself to a plate-sized steak and a slab of dried-apple pie.

Then he set out to find Ray Stone, the dead man's contact here.

The hostler hadn't exactly said where this Ray Stone conducted his business, but the hint about vigilance-committee interest in the man certainly implied that Stone wouldn't maintain business offices in town. Fargo decided to try the seedier saloons first.

He was wrong. Everyone he quietly spoke to admitted to knowing about Stone. But not Stone's whereabouts.

"Him?" one bartender finally said with a snort of disgust. "You wouldn't find him in a place like this. Check the Golden Hind."

"Golden Hind?" Fargo asked. "Sounds like the owner's got an ass made of twenty-four karat."

The bartender snickered but didn't elaborate. Fargo thanked him and left.

It was late by then, nearing midnight, but Bozeman continued to roar. The lamplight along the business streets was as bright as ever, and the boardwalks were full of men. There was even heavy wagon traffic in the dry ruts of the streets. It was a booming camp, full of opportunities for profit. Or for sudden loss.

Fargo passed a drunk who was reeling his way out of an alley mouth, loudly complaining that he'd been robbed. No one on the street paid much attention. They seemed to feel it was his problem and he was welcome to deal with it however he wished. A timid man wouldn't be comfortable here.

The Golden Hind was a small establishment, set back from the street and surrounded by a white picket fence. It looked more like a private club than a regular saloon.

Much of the downstairs portion of the two-story building was taken up by a large room with a polished mahogany bar at one end, tables in the center, and gaming tables laid out at the far end. A staircase led upstairs, presumably to rooms for sleeping or private entertainments. A small stage ringed with carbide footlights and hung with red velvet draperies was at the rear of the big room. The lights were cool now and the stage empty, but a sleeve-gartered "professor" was beside it pumping the pedals of a self-playing piano. Table service was offered by women in short skirts and net stockings.

Pricey kind of place, Fargo thought. But damned interesting all the same.

He went to the bar and ordered a beer. It was delivered in a glass mug and it had just enough head to show quality, not to imply stinginess on the part of the management.

"Ten cents," the barman said. Fargo'd been right. The Golden Hind was damned expensive.

"I'm looking for a fellow." As always, wherever he went, no matter his other interests of the moment, Fargo's eyes were busy roving over the crowd in the place, looking for a face that could lead to the end of his long, long search for the murderers of the Wells Fargo agent who had been Skye Fargo's father.

"One in particular?"

"Stone. I heard he might be here."

The bartender looked not so much at Fargo as behind him, as if satisfying himself that Fargo was alone. "Trouble?"

"No trouble," Fargo said.

"Second floor. Room Five. End of the hall."

"Thanks." Fargo drained off his beer and turned toward the staircase. His progress halted when the piano professor left his machine to light the ring of stage spots, then turned off the player roll and gave a respectable flourish to get the crowd's attention. He already had that, though. There was an air of anticipation in the place. Even the roulette wheel was allowed to spin to a stop and remain silent, no more clickety-clatter of the ball spinning out fortune or loss.

Fargo leaned against the banister at the foot of the stairs and waited to see what the big deal was.

The red velvet drapes were whisked aside, and the footlights revealed one of the loveliest women Fargo had seen in many a month.

His first impression was of size. This was a big woman. Six feet or more tall. There was nothing fat or sloppy about her, though. Big as she was, her body was perfectly proportioned and full enough to make a man hard just from looking at her.

Under the stage makeup and footlights it was difficult to get an accurate idea of her age and coloring except that her hair was as black as Fargo's and her eyes a clear, striking green. Fargo guessed her to be in her thirties, possibly more, unlikely to be less. Not that he—or any of the other panting men who were watching—gave a damn. She was a beauty. A man's fantasies come to glorious life.

Her costume, theatrical though it was, was designed more for promise than display. The bodice was cut low, revealing a hint of full, ripe breast-swell. But revealing only that hint. Showing nothing except in the fevered imagination of the observer. The gown was long, reaching fully to the floor, so that no calf or ankle might be revealed. Her sleeves were long and her hands gloved. This woman, whoever she was, could generate more excitement from behind the protective coverings of cloth than could any number of the now politely still bargirls in their short skirts with half their asses hanging out in the breeze.

No wonder the place had gotten quiet. The other men here must have known what was coming when those lamps were lighted.

The woman gave a slow, confident nod to the guests who were her audience, then another to the piano player.

The professor grinned, poised his curved fingers over the ivories, and then pounced.

No sweet, sad love song this. The man was belting out a hard, hot number.

And, incredibly, the woman belted out a rich, full song to match the music.

Lordy, but she could sing. Fargo could feel the quality of her voice reach down inside him and for just a moment bring him out of himself and into the flow of her song.

That, by damn, was a gift.

He decided that Ray Stone could wait another minute or so. Right now the Trailsman had more interesting things to do.

It was only later, when the spot lights were extinguished that Fargo could tear himself away and climb the stairs to Stone's room.

The door to Number Five was opened by a guy so damned big Fargo found himself looking into the man's Adam's apple. The bodyguard—which was what he almost had to be—was dressed like an undertaker. Black broadcloth suit. Black broadcloth vest. Black string tie. Black derby. The guy bulged with so much muscle he looked like a sausage with a black broadcloth skin on it. His face had been battered and bashed into shapes and textures his mother probably wouldn't have recognized. Probably a has-been prizefighter. He had nice manners, though.

"Who the hell are you?"

"I came to see Stone."

"Why?"

"About things you're too goddamn dumb to understand." Fargo wasn't worried about this big bastard's kind. Not unless Fargo turned stupid himself and let the big guy get his hands on him. Except for that unlikely possibility, though, Fargo could take on a roomful of this type without mussing his hair. You simply ignored the Marquess of Queensberry and blew .44-caliber holes in their guts until they lost interest. Fargo pushed past the bodyguard and went into the room without waiting for an invitation.

Fargo had expected the upstairs rooms to be flocked-velvet playpens where the well-to-do of Bozeman could party in privacy. This room, at least, was set up more like a gentleman's study, with a leather-upholstered couch, a wall of bookshelves, and a broad, handsome desk. Apparently the gentlemen of Bozeman sometimes needed privacy for business deals too.

The man seated at the desk would be Ray Stone. He was dressed like a gentleman. But the resemblance ended there. There was something about him, something in his eyes and the nearly chinless shape of his jaw, that made Fargo think of a wolverine in coat and tie.

"Should I know you?" he asked.

"Not likely. Are you Ray Stone?"

The man nodded.

"I'm looking for someone named Ray. To tell you the truth, I don't know if you're him or not."

"Why are you looking for this, uh, person named Ray?" Stone sat back in his chair. He smiled, but the expression didn't reach his eyes. He folded his hands in his lap, and Fargo noticed that he had put his right hand conveniently close to a vest pocket that held either an almighty big watch or something with some sting in it. Fargo would have bet on a .41-caliber derringer.

"I have a message for him," Fargo said. If Ray Stone had been a different sort of man, Fargo might have laid it out for him. But the dying little man on the *Nellie Nye* had been serious enough about his packet to be thinking about it with his last thoughts this side of hell. Fargo wasn't going to casually drop the oilskin packet on the first Ray he met in Bozeman.

"You haven't told me much, Mr.—?"

"Fargo. Skye Fargo."

Stone's expression took on some interest, and he sat forward in the chair. "I've heard the name."

"Sometimes they call me the Trailsman."

Stone smiled. "You could be a great help to me, Fargo. If what I've heard about you is true. Regardless of what your message is."

"I'm not looking for work right now. This is more like a favor for a friend."

"And what is the message, Mr. Fargo?"

Fargo ignored Stone's question and asked, "Would you have been expecting a messenger up the Missouri, Stone?"

"I might have been."

"A small fellow. Mustache. Side-whiskers. Quiet."

"I might have been," Stone said again.

"That doesn't tell me anything, Mr. Stone. You—"

He never had time to finish the comment.

The conversation ended with the loud crash of splintering wood as someone kicked the door open, shattering the lock and smashing the door back into the face of the big bodyguard.

Men tumbled inside the room, revolvers and pistols leveled, shotgun barrels gaping wickedly.

Every one of them had a flour sack pulled over his head with holes hacked out of the material over their eyes.

Well, dammit, the hostler had said something about that committee. Fargo wished the guy had said a bit about their timing too.

Fargo and Ray Stone raised their hands and tried their best to look inoffensive.

The big bodyguard wasn't so bright. Even when faced by a dozen men or more with guns cocked and drawn, the bodyguard tried to cope by way of his muscle.

The big man roared in fury and launched himself at the nearest three or four vigilantes.

One vigilante—Fargo happened to be watching him at the moment and so saw it clearly—was so startled by the unexpected stupidity of the action that his finger tightened involuntarily on the trigger of the little Smith & Wesson rimfire he was carrying. The little gun discharged, sending its small slug into the butt of the vigilante standing in front of him.

That gunshot was enough to set off the rest of the edgy vigilantes. They turned their guns toward the bodyguard. The combined roar sounded like artillery fire inside the confinement of the room. Fargo's ears would likely be ringing for the next week.

Still, he was in a damn sight better shape than the dumbass bodyguard.

The fellow turned into an instant fountain, pumping bright-red sticky stuff in all directions before the guns even stopped firing.

"You should've hired a better class of help," Fargo suggested to Stone.

Then the vigilantes reached them, grabbed both by the arms, and made short work of stripping their weapons away, Fargo's holstered Colt and the double-decker derringer that Stone had in his pocket.

"Move," a hooded vigilante growled, his voice artificially low as if he didn't want it recognized or remembered.

"Would you mind answering a few questions first?" Fargo asked.

Stone said nothing. He looked almost resigned to the situation. As if he had known it would come eventually. Probably in a state of shock, Fargo decided.

The vigilantes continued to press their way into the overcrowded room. It wasn't a particularly hopeful sign that the late-comers were carrying coils of rope with them.

Maybe, Fargo thought, he would have a chance to talk with them during the trial—if they went in for that sort of conscience-relieving activity—or at least on the way to wherever the hangings were supposed to take place. Hell, there had to be *one* decent man among them. That was what vigilance committees were supposed to be, the decent men of a community. Wasn't it?

Shit!

Maybe not in Bozeman. Not as decent as Skye Fargo would have liked, anyhow.

Accompanied by grunts and growls of unspoken instruction, the rope was brought forward; it had a thirteen-knot noose already fashioned at the end of the coil.

Without any threats or bullying or mistreatment—but without any damn discussion either—the vigilante with the rope stuck the noose over Ray Stone's head and pulled it tight, taking care to position the bulky knot properly beneath Stone's ear so that the knot would snap Stone's spinal cord and give him a quick, clean death when he hit the end of his rope.

Considerate as all shit, Fargo thought. Decent of them.

The free end of the rope was tied to a steam pipe that fed the radiator in the corner, and someone opened the window. By then more vigilantes had Stone's hands tied behind his back.

Vigilante hands picked Stone up, and someone tied his ankles tight together.

"Ready?"

The hoods nodded.

Then they threw Ray Stone out of the second-floor window.

There was a faint, muffled pop as Stone's neck broke and a wet, fluttery sound as his bowels emptied themselves. The rope pulled taut over the sill.

Interesting how ugly a damn rope could be. Fargo noticed how the steam pipe had bowed slightly from the strain placed on it. He didn't know why he bothered to look at that, but the new curve pulled into the pipe seemed to fascinate him.

Without another word the hooded men turned toward Fargo, and another man with another rope stepped forward. This rope, too, had the thirteen turns built into the knot. It was not in the least bit comforting to see that the Bozeman vigilantes knew how to do their work.

The vigilantes came toward him.

Skye Fargo took a deep breath. What the fuck.

With a scream of defiance he began to kick and bite and twist for all he was worth.

"Tom! Jason! Quit that." The voice was low, firm, and very much in control. It was also very much a woman's voice.

Tom and Jason, if that was who they were behind the masks, quit what they were doing. Fargo didn't mind. Tom and Jason and the boys had given up on the business-like efficiency they had displayed toward Ray Stone and had been busy beating the hell out of the Trailsman.

"Dammit, Glenna . . ." The voice sounded muffled by the flour-sack hood but still peeved.

"Oh, hush, Tom. Everybody knows who you are. I certainly don't care." She came further into the room, acting sure of herself amid this crowd of armed and dangerous men.

Fargo managed to turn his head far enough to see her. Which was not as easy as it sounded. There was very little about him at this point that seemed capable of working the way it was supposed to.

The woman who had interrupted things was the same beauty who'd been singing downstairs not half an hour ago. She must have been changing out of her stage gown just before she entered the room, because now she was wearing a long Chinese red silk dressing gown and boa-trimmed mules.

Fargo thought she was just about the most beautiful thing he'd seen lately. He was willing to listen to what this Glenna had to say. Apparently the vigilantes were too.

"Jason, Barry," she ordered. "Take the gentleman down the hall to my private quarters. Don't just stand there looking at me like that. Do what I told you."

"But, Glenna—"

"Pish," Glenna said. "This man is no more one of Stone's people than I am."

"But—" one of the vigilantes tried again.

"Let him go," she ordered, her tone of voice hard this time, no mistaking her seriousness.

Incredibly, the vigilantes—all half-dozen or so of them who had hold of him—let go.

Fargo fell back against the polished hardwood floor, cracking his head painfully but under the circumstances not really minding that small bit of hurt.

"You don't know anything about this man, Glenna," one of the vigilantes protested.

"More than you do, Tom," she said. "You trusted my information enough when I was telling you about Ray Stone. I know something about Mr. Fargo here from the same source."

"Well, in that case—"

"Now do as I say, Tom. Let me handle this." She

seemed to assume that the subject of Skye Fargo and his future was quite closed now as far as the Bozeman vigilance committee was concerned. Once again she directed Jason and Barry—Fargo had no idea what any of them looked like behind their hoods, but Glenna was having no difficulty whatsoever in identifying the men—to help Fargo down the hall to Glenna's rooms. Two of the hooded men moved to obey, and Glenna began giving instructions about the disposition of the two bodies, those of Stone and his bodyguard.

Helluva woman, Fargo thought woozily as the two men who had just been bent on killing him now picked him up and supported his arms across their shoulders as they dragged him out of the room and down the hall.

"Thanks," Fargo said. He accepted the tiny glass of French brandy that Glenna handed him. She poured one for herself and carried it behind a dressing screen set in the corner of the huge, beautifully furnished bed/sitting room.

"I apologize for the inconvenience, Mr. Fargo."

He could not see her, but her voice reached him clearly from the other side of the screen. He could also hear small movements and an occasional rustle of cloth.

"Inconvenience," he repeated. "Interesting way to put it, that." He heard a low chuckle from behind the screen. "Mind if I ask you a few questions?"

"Not at all, Mr. Fargo."

"That right there is one of them," he said. "You knowin' my name. Miss Glenna, you and me've never met before. Believe me, I'd remember if we had."

She laughed again. "Should I take that as a compliment?"

"Sure. Also the truth. But you know my name. And that I wasn't a part of whatever Stone got himself hanged for."

"Just a moment, Mr. Fargo." There was more noise

from behind the screen—small sounds, a period of silence—then Glenna returned to view, fully dressed now and with her brandy in hand.

She was even more attractive than she had seemed on the stage. Her heavy footlight makeup had been removed and her hair redone into a softer style. She was a damned beauty, no question about it.

She pulled a fragile-looking armchair close to the love seat where Fargo was, and set her glass on the table.

She was in no hurry. She reached for the cut-glass decanter and refilled their glasses before she spoke again. 'There is less mystery here than you might think," she said. "Did you happen to notice the heat register in the floor beside the desk in that room?"

"Should I have?"

She smiled. "Of course not. Which is the beauty of it. My dressing room is directly below the office of the late Mr. Stone. And I, sir, am an inveterate eavesdropper."

"Really?" Fargo took a sip of the brandy. Pretty good stuff.

"By . . . how shall I put this? Not from idle meanness, Mr. Fargo. It is a part of my activities here. With good and just reason that I needn't explain to you, sir. Call it simply your very good fortune that I happened to be listening when you were speaking with Mr. Stone. That is how I learned your name. And, uh, certain other things of interest to me."

"Certain other things?" Fargo was damned curious now.

Glenna shrugged and admitted. "It endangers me to have you here and to make these explanations to you, Mr. Fargo. I hope you appreciate that."

Skye Fargo had no idea what this woman was talking about. He didn't object to her interference on his behalf, mind. But he didn't know what her point was.

"You were trying to deliver a message to Mr. Stone under the mistaken belief that he was the Ray that gentleman referred to."

Fargo gave her a questioning look and raised the tiny glass to his lips again.

"The gentleman, whose name you didn't give, was a Mr. Scott Paine, Mr. Fargo. Mr. Paine was—I must assume he is dead or the message would not have been relayed through you—Mr. Paine was an agent of the Treasury Department. He was enroute to Bozeman, Mr. Fargo, to deliver certain, uh, instructions. To me. I must have that message, Mr. Fargo. That is the reason I interfered with the vigilance committee. You must give me the message."

"Must?" Fargo asked. "Strong word, Miss Glenna. Maybe I don't 'must' do everything you think I do."

Glenna opened a drawer at the front of the little table that was between her chair and Fargo's seat. She pulled out a handbag and laid it in her lap. Without any particular urgency she opened the bag and reached into it.

Smiling now, she removed a nickel-plated Sharps Ace four-barreled derringer, a rimfire model of small caliber but potentially deadly effect, and placed it in her lap.

Aw, shit, Fargo thought. Out of one frying pan and into a next-door fire.

"Don't you think we oughta talk this over some?" he asked.

Instead of shooting him, Glenna pulled the drawstring of the handbag closed and tossed the purse to him. She kept the little gambler's gun in her lap, however, where she could reach it if she wanted.

Fargo caught the handbag and gave her an inquiring look.

"Inside," she said. "There is a silver case with a mirror in it. Open that."

Obediently—this didn't seem like a good time to get balky with her—Fargo rooted through the odds and ends of junk that ladies carry in their purses until he found the engraved silver case. He opened it.

"Look behind the mirror," she told him.

It took him a moment of fumbling to pry the quicksilvered glass out of its frame. Hidden behind the mirror there was a piece of pasteboard that originally had had a rectangular shape and had been cut down to fit the compact. The card identified the bearer as Glenna Marie Raye, an employee of the Secret Service, United States Treasury Department.

"Well I'll be damned," Fargo said.

Glenna Raye smiled. "I wouldn't know about that, Mr. Fargo. I do know that Mr. Paine was coming here to see me."

"What is this all about?"

"Are you suggesting, sir, that you will not deliver the message without that information?"

It was Fargo's turn to smile. He was feeling considerably easier about the situation now. It was, after all, improbable that government employees would turn to idle murder.

"No," he told her honestly enough. "I'm just a naturally curious man, I reckon." He reached into his pocket and found the oilskin-wrapped packet he had taken from the dying man back on the *Nellie Nye*. He handed her both her purse and the packet. "That's what I was asked to deliver. There wasn't any other message. Paine, if that's what his name was, was dying at the time. We didn't have much chance to talk things over."

"Thank you, Mr. Fargo."

"He hadn't even time to get it out that it was a woman he wanted the thing taken to, nor that Raye was a last name. He just said Ray, and I assumed . . . Well, you likely know what I assumed."

"Yes." Miss Raye tucked the packet into the bodice of her gown without examining it, probably unwilling to open it in a stranger's presence.

"I am somewhat in your power here, Mr. Fargo. I hope you shan't take advantage of that."

"I don't understand that. Or much of anything else that's going on here, Miss Raye."

She sighed. "I suppose some explanation is necessary. You are no doubt aware of the growing political, uh, dissatisfactions back East?"

"Not really," the Trailsman said. "I'm a westerner through and through. I don't know much about that kind of thing, and truth to tell, I don't all that much care. We have our own problems out here without taking on someone else's."

"Yes, well, not everyone feels the same. And in truth I cannot say that I understand your attitude, Mr. Fargo, any more than you seem to understand mine. Regardless, there may be a conflict between the states of this nation. I pray that that will not happen, but it may. If it does, there will very likely be a great need for gold to finance any hostilities which might occur. The disloyal opposition would be interested in obtaining the products of distant western gold mines for their own ends. And naturally enough, the Treasury Department is determined that such a thing mustn't happen. I won't go into details about why I am here now or what Paine's role in it would have been. Suffice it to say, Mr. Fargo, that we are here in our government's lawful service. And that I would much prefer that my employment be not known."

"You're a spy," Fargo said, boiling it down to simpler terms.

"That isn't a very nice way to put it."

Fargo shrugged. "You were spying on Stone through that heat register. Come to think of it, from what I heard in that room, the vigilance committee got their information about Stone from you. You said yourself you'd've let them hang me if it hadn't been for the information you wanted from me."

"I delivered no false information about Stone, if that is what you are thinking," Glenna said. She was right. It was exactly what Fargo was wondering now. "Stone and his men were organizing parties of raiders to prey on freight traffic moving to and from the mining camps in the territory. If they had motives that went beyond personal gain, that doesn't alter the fact that they were repeatedly committing robbery and murder. I admit that I exposed them to the committee. If I had motives beyond the obvious ones of maintaining law and order in this territory, well, surely that should have no bearing on the matter."

"I'll have to think about that one some," Fargo said. He finished off his brandy and started to rise.

"Mr. Fargo."

"Miss Raye?"

"My life would be forfeit if certain, uh, parties, not only here but in other parts of the territory as well, were to discover that I am not merely the singer they believe me to be."

"I won't say anything," Fargo promised. "That'd be a helluva poor way to repay you for saving me from a hanging." Again he tried to rise, but again Glenna stayed him.

"You are a handsome man, Mr. Trailsman," she said.

"Thanks." He looked at her more closely. Damn, but she was something. A big, fine-looking woman, the kind that could raise a sweat on a man just by being in the same room with him.

Was this an offer? he was wondering. And if it was, was it because she was really interested? Or just because she wanted to put some personal-type chains on him to keep him in line?

Fargo chuckled. The next question was . . . Who the hell cared? If this beautiful woman wanted to go climb into that bed he couldn't help but keep noticing on the other side of the room, well . . . why not? Whatever her reasons.

"Yes, Mr. Fargo?"

"I think," he said, "it's time you and me dropped this mister-and-miss nonsense."

This time she didn't stop him when he rose from the love seat to lean over her chair and lower his lips to hers.

Glenna's mouth opened to his, and her tongue probed deliciously forward.

Fargo felt a shiver of pleasure roving up and down his spine as Glenna Raye responded to him with a degree of ardor that was every bit as powerful as her song had been.

Her hand found him, and he heard a groan. It took him a moment to realize that the sound had come from his own throat.

He bent, slid an arm under her knees, and lifted her into his arms. He turned, carrying her, toward the waiting bed.

4

Fargo knew he was close to Virginia City when the thick growth of low conifers gave way to mud and sap-stained stumps and the litter of dying slash. Mining operations took a hell of a lot of timber, and a camp of any size could denude the earth for miles around it.

He let the big Ovaro make his way along the road without conscious direction. He was thinking about the tasks that lay ahead, still unsure whether he should have accepted Glenna Raye's chore. She had asked it as a favor, really. And her method of prepayment had certainly been worthwhile. It was a simple-enough thing, and one she trusted him with if only because he had already become involved, more or less, so one more small favor hardly seemed out of line. Besides, she said the man he was to deliver her note to might be able to help him in his search for Margaret Anne Fitzroy. No need for secrecy about that, so he had felt no reluctance in telling Glenna about it.

He did, however, feel a little uncomfortable taking on the job of a spy's courier, no matter if it was only a casual thing done as a favor.

Still, he didn't see what harm could come of it.

He took the pinto into Virginia City on the well-marked

road from Bozeman and found the town to be a smaller and much rougher proposition than the longer-established Bozeman had been. New, raw, and booming. Thrown into being by the discovery of gold.

Gold camps were not among the Trailsman's favorite places. Crazy people flocked to them by the hundreds, men who might once have been perfectly sane and ordinary but whose eyes glazed with greed once they heard of another new strike in another new camp. The places popped into being like mushrooms after a spring shower and frequently were no longer inhabited. They brought mobs into country that was empty until their coming, and changed the face of the earth almost overnight.

Helluva thing when you thought about it.

Virginia City was like most of them, busy as an anthill, ugly as sin, and day and night the sound of the stamp mills beating out the rhythm of the tune called Money.

Fargo found a place to stable the Ovaro. He didn't trust the management quite so much here as he had at the place back in Bozeman. Still, this one seemed the best Virginia City had to offer. At least it didn't look likely to fall down. The barn was built of timbers, which meant it had been here from near the beginning. The newer buildings in town were made of lumber, which meant that a sawmill had opened and someone was making his fortune aboveground.

"I'll pay you the full board," Fargo told the hostler, "but I'll be back to do the tending myself. And don't let anybody but me close to him. I set store by that animal."

"Whatever you say." The hostler sounded like he didn't give a damn what happened to man or beast so long as he had his bottle and wasn't bothered. He uncorked the pint jug and took a swallow without offering a drink to his customer.

"That's what I say," Fargo told him. He'd go find

someone else to get directions from. He wouldn't trust this old coot to give him directions to daylight.

The thought of a drink wasn't bad after the trip down from Bozeman, so he took the main street toward the business district and stopped in at the first saloon he saw.

"I could use a beer and the answer to a question."

"The beer I can handle. Don't know about the question till I hear what it is," the barman said. He drew a short beer, half-head, but spilled off most of the foam and refilled the mug before he handed it over. "Five cents for the beer. No charge for that question."

"I'm looking for a man named Maharky. You know him?"

"Sure, everybody knows Maharky. Except most call him Malarky. Full o' shit as a Christmas goose, but he's harmless. Always giving advice about everything under the goddamn sun. Likable cuss, though. Everybody gets along with Malarky." The bartender thought for a moment. "This time o' day you'd prob'ly find him over at the Stope."

"He works there?"

"Hell, I don't know of anybody'd hire Malarky for actual money. He claims he's one of them engineers, but everybody knows better."

"Thanks." Fargo was in no hurry. He enjoyed the beer and a bite from the free-lunch spread, then another beer before he left.

The Stope was a cavernous, high-ceilinged place—probably how it got its name—that looked like it had been a barn before it was turned into a saloon. There was more than enough room overhead for a second floor although none had been built.

Fargo bought himself another beer as his price of admission. "Know a man named Maharky?" The barman pointed toward a trio of men standing at the other end of the bar. It took no great powers of deduction to figure out which would be Fargo's—Glenna's, really—man.

Two of the talkers were well-set-up, prosperous-looking gentlemen who might have been mine owners or genuine engineers. The third was a smallish fellow in a threadbare suit of clothes and a derby that should have been discarded years ago.

Fargo drifted down the bar toward them. "Mr. Maharky?"

"Yes?"

"I wonder if I could have a word with you when you're free."

Maharky beamed with pleasure. "But of course, son. If these gentlemen could excuse us?"

The gentlemen seemed only too happy to do so.

"We've been discussing deep-shaft-pump extraction methods." Maharky chattered as he led Fargo aside.

There was something about Maharky—a certain rheumy wetness in his eyes, perhaps a vagueness of expression—that hinted that he lacked some of the vital facilities.

Not that he was a half-wit. Not quite. Just that the spark of reason had been extinguished.

Fargo couldn't quite pinpoint the lack, but he recognized it. He questioned whether this was really the man Glenna Raye had sent him to.

"Uh, I may have the wrong man, Mr. Maharky. Is there, uh, another Maharky in town?"

"Oh, you've come to the right man, sir. Honus Maharky, expert counsel on mining affairs, both hard rock and soft. Expert witness in courts of law. Oh, yes indeed. You've come to the right man, sir."

Fargo noticed that Maharky's lips were slack. A bit of spittle had collected at the corner of his mouth. Looking at it, wanting to wipe it off for the man, was distinctly uncomfortable. Fargo had to look away and pretend to examine a poorly mounted deer head on the wall to avoid staring at it.

"And what is the nature of your business, sir? D'you want to hire me as consultant on your claim? My fees are reasonable, I assure you. Highly reasonable, but worth far more than the price. Inestimable value, in fact." Maharky was grinning vacantly. The glob of spittle remained.

"I, uh, I wanted to see a gentleman named Maharky about, uh, a certain Miss Raye."

Maharky's eyes focused sharp and clear, all the vagueness gone so quickly that Fargo wasn't sure he had actually seen it happen. Maharky's eyes cut sideways to survey the rest of the people in the saloon, assured himself that no one was paying attention, and returned his gaze to Skye Fargo. His mouth remained slack and foolish, but there was a clear, penetrating intelligence in those pale eyes now. If Fargo hadn't witnessed the change, he wouldn't have believed it. From any distance away, though, the alteration wouldn't have been at all noticeable.

"We'll talk some business then, sir. But not here. Come up to my room. I've charts an' graphs I can show you. My bona fides, if you please. Proof of my efficacy as your consultant, sir." The voice had an inane, whining quality about it, the nattering sound of a 'fool. The eyes now, though, said otherwise.

"Of course, Mr. Maharky."

Maharky laughed. It sounded almost like a giggle. "Y'can call me Malarky. Everybody does."

"Yes," Fargo said. "I'm sure they do."

Honus Maharky, it seemed, was a master of the actor's craft. Fargo wondered why he was here doing this lonely job when the man could have made a fortune on the stage.

Fargo followed him to the privacy of his tiny, pigsty room and delivered the sealed packet Glenna had entrusted to him. Here, behind the walls of the cubicle that was his home, Maharky allowed himself to stand straighter and let a bit more of his true self show through to someone who already knew his secret. Fargo was well impressed.

"No verbal messages?" Maharky asked in a crisp tone.

"None." Fargo hesitated. "There is one thing."

"Yes?"

"Glenna said you might be able to do me a service. Help me find someone who lives here. Or used to."

Maharky grinned. There was no spittle on his lips now, and his jaw was firm. "Possible. The village idiot hears more than people tend to realize."

Fargo laughed. "And I suspect that the village idiot is damned good at his job."

Maharky chuckled and bowed low with dignity and grace.

Fargo briefly explained who he was seeking, but not why. The real Maharky wasn't the sort who'd require lengthy explanation.

Maharky closed his eyes for a moment, his shoulders tense, and thought about it.

"Powell," he said slowly. "I remember a Donnie Powell. Came here early. Died and left a widow. She also died."

"Here?"

"Yes. Both graves are here. I have no idea if they are marked. And of course there has been no registration of births or deaths. We are not strong on the civilized amenities here."

"It's the daughter I'm looking for," Fargo said.

"The daughter. So you said. But I'm afraid my attentions haven't been on quite, uh, every resident. If you understand. Let me see. . . ." He thought for quite a while but finally shook his head. "I know nothing at all about a daughter. Would it help you if I asked around?"

Maharky didn't seem to mind taking on a favor for the

Trailsman. In fact, he sounded positively eager to do so. Fargo got the impression that Mr. Honus Maharky had a thoroughly good time discovering things.

"I'd appreciate that, Mr. Maharky. I'll be in town for a few days. If you do learn anything, I'd like to know, of course."

Maharky laughed. "Please do remember to call me Malarky, Fargo. Anything else would confuse people."

Fargo smiled at him. "If that's what you want."

"Goodness, yes, Fargo. I have a reputation to uphold, you know," he said happily.

Damned strange little man, Fargo thought as he left Maharky's shabby quarters and went to find a room for himself.

"Want some comp'ny, honey? A little something warm to get close to?"

A *little* something? The overpainted whore probably outweighed Fargo by thirty pounds. She'd have overflowed a circus tent, never mind the skimpy costume she had somehow stuffed herself into.

"No, thanks," Fargo said. He reached for his drink and tried to ignore her, but for some reason the damn woman had got it in mind that he should be her next customer, and she wasn't willing to let it go at that.

"Aw, c'mon, honey. Buy me a drink anyhow. Just one li'l drinkee." She leaned close and nibbled at his right ear. Her armpits had a sour smell hanging in the air around them, and her breath wasn't something to brag about. Even so, Fargo tried to be polite to her. Hell, she was a human being.

"I'm sorry," he said, "but I'm one broke son of a bitch, and I know a lady as fine and fancy as you are, well, there's just no way I could afford your time."

She giggled, immensely pleased with the compliment.

Unfortunately, though, his protestations about being broke did not deter her.

"Aren't you the gennulmun, now. Such a pretty fella." She ran her hand up and down his arm, feeling his muscles and making calf's eyes at him.

"Look, lady, really I can't—"

"Get your fuckin' hands off my woman," a male voice roared behind Fargo.

Oh, shit, Fargo thought.

He turned, quite willing to relinquish the bawd to the other man. Hell, he'd almost be willing to pay the other guy just to take the fat whore off him.

"Look, mister—"

"Damn you, Charlie," the whore screamed. "Don't you be buttin' in here. Find me a fine-lookin' man like this han'some feller here, an' what happens. You gotta come along an' spoil everything. You always spoil everything, thinkin' you own a girl, thinkin' you should ought to have me all to yourself. It ain't fair, Charlie," she wailed.

She'd started out angry; now she sounded sad. She began to cry.

"Aw, sweetie. Don' you take on like that." Charlie, who looked like the bastard offspring of an ox crossed on a hairball—big and covered with thick fur over nearly every visible surface—came forward and put an arm tenderly around the fat whore's shoulders. He kissed her on the cheek and patted her.

The look he gave her was disgustingly sweet. The look he gave Fargo once the whore had been gentled was just . . . disgusting.

"You leave be, hear?"

"Of course, friend. I didn't know the, uh, lady was spoken for." Fargo smiled, amused at the two of them and definitely far from being jealous.

Charlie grunted, uncertain of whether to take it further or

not. He petted the fat woman some more and glowered a little.

"You really do care, don't you, Charlie?"

" 'Course I care, honeybunch." Charlie bent low to reach the whore's cheek and give her another peck.

Fargo took advantage of the distraction to pick up his drink and carry it down to the other end of the bar. The man beside him there gave Fargo a wide-eyed, straight-faced look and said, "You missed out, friend. Old Frenchy there is about the best this place offers."

"Yeah. My tough luck, I guess."

The fellow grinned and raised his glass to Fargo in a silent toast.

"Buy you a refill?" Fargo offered.

"Now, that's an offer a wise man never refuses. I accept and thank you kindly."

Fargo motioned to get the bartender's attention and pointed to the two glasses. The barman was quick with the refills.

"You're a new face in the crowd," the friendly drinker said. "Just in?"

"Uh huh. Looking for a girl."

"Aren't we all?"

Fargo smiled. "So we are. But I'm looking for a partic-ular girl. Used to live here, I'm told."

The man shook his head. "If a fella can't be satisfied with a fine-looker like Frenchy you must be hard to please."

"It's a curse, I know. But what can I tell you? I'm picky."

The man grinned. "Yeah, well, anyhow, tell me your troubles and I'll see if I can help. I pride myself on being something of an expert on the shady ladies and the eligible debutantes of Virginia City."

"The girl I'm looking for is named Margaret Anne

Fitzroy, but she could have been calling herself Powell after her stepfather. Redheaded girl, I'm told."

"Powell. Mmm. That kinda rings a bell. I remember a man named Powell. But I don't recall any girl in that family."

"Really?"

"Yeah. Let's see. Donnie, right?"

Fargo nodded.

"Sure. Donnie Powell. Worked for the Bailey Number Three till some shoring let loose half a mountain on him. Yeah, I remember him now. Mean son of a bitch, even if I do say it about the dead."

"But you don't remember him having a daughter with him?"

The man thought for a moment and shook his head. "No. No kid. Had him a woman. I remember her. Scrawny, thin little woman. Looked all the time like she was 'most wore out. Lot of bruises on her, I'd bet. Where they don't show. If you know what I mean."

"You did say he was a mean one," Fargo said.

"Yeah. Low-down mean. But sneaky about it. He wouldn't stand up to a man, but I think he was the kind that would beat up on a woman. Scared of anybody that could hit back, but wasn't afraid to take it out on anybody who couldn't. You know?"

"I know the type."

"Nobody minded much when he got his. Some pretty good boys died in that cave-in with him, though. His fault, the way I hear it. He was in charge of the shoring. The pity was the fellas he took with him."

"I know what you mean."

"But I sure don't remember anything about him having a kid." The man thought for another moment and affirmed the memory with a shake of his head. "Nope, nothing like that." He grinned. "An' I'd remember a redhead for sure.

I got a thing about redheads, especially the natural kind, with red hair top and bottom both. Only one like that I've had was right here in Virginia City. Whee-ew, was she some! She could throw a man's back plumb out of joint. And make him want to come back for another treatment of the same.''

He nodded down the bar toward where Frenchy and Charlie were still billing and cooing over each other, Charlie now squeezing Frenchy's big ass in his almost-as-big paw.

''That ladyfriend of yours down there, a man can have himself some of that if he's desperate enough and has fifty cents to spend. The girls over on the line, they go for as much as five dollars apiece. This redheaded Annie, she charged ten dollars. Ten Ewe Ess dollars, if you can believe it. And had all the business she could handle.''

The man sighed wistfully. ''I got up the nerve and the cash just twice, friend. But I'll never forget them two times, you better believe it. If I had the chance, I'd do it all over again.''

''If you had the chance?'' Fargo asked idly. He was watching Charlie trying to be coy about luring Frenchy up the stairs.

''Yeah. Annie was too fancy for the likes of a place like this. Not enough money here for her. She took off south someplace. I heard tell she was headed for the big money camps down in Colorado. Central City, Golden, someplace like that.'' He sighed again. ''Almost be worth the trip down there if that's true, just to jump in bed with that one one more time.'' He laughed. ''Except, if I could find the money to get there, I couldn't afford Annie's price once I did. Bet she's charging fifty bucks by now. And worth it. That's the thing, friend. I'd say that she's worth it.'' The fellow straightened and grinned. ''Say, now, this talk's too serious for a wet night. My turn to buy the refills.''

''And my pleasure to accept,'' Fargo said. He drained his glass while his newfound drinking pal waved the bartender to them.

It was a scene Fargo was to play over and over. Everybody in the damned town remembered Donnie Powell. At least everyone Fargo talked to. A few remembered his wife. No one had any recollection of a daughter with them.

Damned strange, Fargo thought. You'd think that a redheaded girl would make an impression on the woman-starved men of a mining camp, but this one hadn't. So much for logical thinking.

He kept looking. He quit asking men and tried talking with the decent women of the community. There weren't so very many of them and surprisingly few of them were unwilling to talk with a handsome stranger.

Several, in fact, were downright accommodating. Above and beyond the limits of what Fargo would have expected from the ''decent'' set.

Matter of fact, some of those respectable ladies, who would have gasped out loud and fainted dead away if they so much as passed a soiled woman on the street, were capable of teaching professional tricks to the girls on the line. As Fargo had occasion to discover. This particular trail wasn't hard to put up with at times.

He was becoming discouraged, though. Fitzroy wasn't paying him to enjoy afternoon romps with the good ladies of Virginia City.

The man wanted to find his daughter, and that was weighing on the Trailsman. The more he looked and the less he learned, the more personal this search was becoming for him.

At odd, unexpected moments he kept having flashbacks of memory. Thoughts of his own family. The pain of knowing he himself would never have the chance he wanted to give to Fitzroy: reunion with the people he most loved and admired in this world.

You'd think that after all this time the memory of them would be blurred, the pain of the loss eased. It wasn't so. He could still see them clearly in his mind's eye. He wished he couldn't. Almost invariably the scene that came to him in sharp, painful clarity was that last time he had seen them.

He'd come home that day and found them dead. Shot to death. Slaughtered. He could still smell the blood and the lingering, sour scent of burnt gunpowder in the home they had shared as a family.

Forget? Skye Fargo almost wished he could. Except then he might be willing to forget also the men he sought. The men who had killed his family.

In the meantime, though, he could hope to find Margaret Fitzroy. He could hope to give Fitzroy the joy of family that would forever be denied to the Trailsman.

His fourth day in Virginia City, discouragement beginning to pull at him, he was currying the Ovaro when Honus Maharky breezed into the livery with his slack jaw and watery eyes, grinning and chattering and making a nuisance of himself.

Maharky spent several minutes extolling his own expertise with horseflesh in general and pack mules in particular, gave a lengthy dissertation on the prevention of harness galls, and then began instructing the sour hostler on the finer points of running a public stable.

The hostler put up with it until his eyes began to glaze, then rudely turned and got the hell out of the barn at a pace just short of a run.

Maharky watched the man out of sight and laughed. "Took him long enough."

Fargo got the impression that Maharky was laughing more at himself than at the hostler, though. "Remind me never to take you lightly," Fargo told the sharp little government spy.

"Why not?" Maharky asked with false innocence. "Everyone else does."

"Yes. So I notice." Fargo's tone was dry.

"I haven't been able to learn much about your missing girl," Maharky said.

"If you've learned anything at all," Fargo said, "it's more than I've turned. I've talked to everybody I could think of. Learned nothing. It's strange, really. Everybody around remembers Powell. Like you did. Not so many the mother. Nobody the girl."

Maharky grunted. "Very much my own experience," he said. "Until I quit asking about Powell's daughter and began asking about a redhaired girl who would have been in Virginia City about the time the Powells arrived here."

Fargo's interest perked up. "Did you do any good?"

"Possibly. Quite possibly." The words were modest enough, but Maharky sounded quite pleased with himself. A workman's pride, Fargo thought. More power to him, though. Skye Fargo wasn't so proud that he'd refuse assistance from an expert. And he was more and more believing that Mr. Honus Maharky was indeed an expert in his chosen field.

"Well?" Fargo prompted.

"There was a redhaired girl who used to live here. She called herself Anne Roy." Maharky smiled. "Sound likely to you?"

"Hell yes," Fargo agreed.

"My thoughts also." Maharky checked behind him to make sure no one was near who would notice that he was acting out of character for the moment. But the barn was empty save for himself, Fargo, and a few horses. "Margaret Anne Fitzroy could become Anne Roy quite easily."

"Is she still here?" Fargo was so anxious that he could feel a thrill of pleasure on Fitzroy's behalf. That reunion could be no more than a telegraph message away.

"No," Maharky said, "but you shouldn't have much difficulty finding her now that you know the name she's using."

"But do you know . . . ?"

"Close. Not specifically, but close enough." Maharky drew out his pleasure in showing off his knowledge by taking the time to fish a cigar butt out of his coat pocket and light the thing.

Fargo found himself too amused by this display to become impatient with the little man. He waited, letting Maharky get it out in his own time and to his own satisfaction.

"Anne Roy left here December last. Bound for Georgetown in Colorado Territory." He grinned. "I got that from the Butterfield agent who sold her the ticket. She paid cash, in coin, if it matters." Maharky sounded quite, quite pleased with himself. And no wonder, Fargo conceded. He had earned it, Fargo agreed.

"Quite a fetching young woman," Maharky added. "The station master remembers her with, um, extreme pleasure. And that from a mere glimpse of her behind her veil." Maharky rolled his eyes skyward and grinned.

"You're a sham and a charlatan, Mr. Maharky. But I salute you," Fargo said with a grin.

Maharky, though, was no longer the bright, enthused discoverer of secrets. Now he was once again the bumbling, sputtering nuisance of Virginia City.

Fargo glanced over his shoulder. The hostler was coming back into the barn, although he looked perfectly willing to turn and run again if Maharky came his way a second time in a single day.

"I'm sorry," Fargo said loudly enough for the hostler to hear, "but my plans have changed. I'll be leaving tomorrow."

Maharky followed him out of the livery, annoying him every step of the way with a constant patter of drivel about mining properties and hard-rock drilling methods.

5

"You're Fargo? Guy they call the Trailsman? Hell, yes, you can join us, and mighty welcome too. We can always use an extry gun anyhow. My pleasure, Fargo." The freighter stuck his hand forward and Fargo shook with him.

It was all right traveling alone. But in country like they'd be passing through, traveling with a party was better. Safer. After all, a man can reload his guns only so fast, and alone he could have his whole day ruined by a party of Sioux or roving Absarokas.

Not that lonely travel meant instant death. Far from it. But a man never knew.

The route they would take wasn't an easy one. There was no easy road from Virginia City down across great, empty Wyoming to the gold digs north of Pikes Peak. If Fargo had been making it alone, he likely would have cut south through Coulter's Hell and down along the Wind River range. The freighter, though, intended to take the longer but safer road east past the Absaroka range, then south along the eastern slope of the Big Horns, to Fort Laramie on the Oregon Trail. From there Fargo would go on alone down to Cherry Creek and the South Platte

River. The South Platte and the mountain streams that fed it had been found to contain a bonanza of placer nuggets, and even more productive were the lodes that had fed that placer gravel over the centuries. It was to this gold-rich country that Anne Roy had apparently gone. Skye Fargo intended to follow her and find out.

The bullwhackers pulled out well before dawn, a train of huge freight wagons, each wagon drawing at least one heavy trailer, each massive rig pulled by a team of sixteen Missouri mules. The freighters regarded themselves as the lords of the prairies, ruling over their domain with long whips and a command of cusswords that approached artistry. A bullwhacker who couldn't cuss up the standards of his peers wasn't well thought of, no matter if he could pop flies out of midair with his twenty-foot blacksnake. Fargo enjoyed the company of the freighters even if he did recognize the limitations they imposed on themselves by following the tried and true roads and shying away from real adventure.

Traveling with a freight string was much like living in a movable town. Spare draft animals had to be brought along in case of need. Each wagon and set of trailers had a near mob of handlers to drive the mules, tend the lines, grease the axles, and perform all the complicated tasks of moving freight over great distances.

Not that there was so very much to be hauled south from the Montana fields. Most goods still traveled to the camps, not away from them.

This train was carrying an entire stamp mill south to the burgeoning Colorado camps. A heavily capitalized Virginia City mine played out and went belly up. Its investors were trying to get something back by selling the mill off to new ownership in the active Colorado fields.

It never ceased to amaze the Trailsman how much a good freighter could haul. The mill's boilers had been taken apart, great, massive slabs of curved iron that resembled nothing but a pile of scrap until reassembled.

The entire mill save for the buildings was there. Gears, rollers, valves, belts, the steel stamp-feet that would pulverize solid rock and turn it into gold-bearing dust that could be separated into concentrates, even the brass steam whistle that would call the mill crew to work. The whole damn thing was there, loaded onto Bill Chatham's wagons.

"We aren't expecting any trouble," Chatham told him. "Leastways, we haven't heard of anything going right now except the usual. Wouldn't hurt, though, if you was to ride point for us. Kinda roam around in front o' the train and keep an eye on things."

"All right." It was the sort of thing Fargo would have done anyway, with or without Chatham's approval.

The first leg of the trip was as safe as a man could hope to expect in this uncertain country. The Crows, the tribe for which the Absaroka Mountains had taken their name, had mostly withdrawn in the face of a constant influx of white miners and soldiers and freighters.

They passed south of Bozeman—Fargo felt no particular desire to return there and have another talk with the local vigilance committee—and swung down into Sioux country.

The Sioux were unpredictable. Fargo wasn't ashamed of his own measure of Indian blood, but having bloodlines in common wouldn't stop the Sioux if they took a notion to count coup on a white wagon train. If a Sioux warrior decided it was a good day to die, there would be no stopping him short of giving him his wish and helping him die. Yet tomorrow that same warrior might be friendly as a pup and willing to trade, share a pipe, play a few games of Hand, share his woman if he had one handy. You just never knew.

The Big Horn Mountains formed a wall to the west of

74

the slow-moving train as the Trailsman scouted the rutted road in advance of the wagons.

There was plenty of sign indicating that some tribe was in the area, but no hint of who they were or what they were up to. With luck, though, the train would make the whole journey south and never see an Indian. Seeing sign didn't bother anyone. It was only the sight of red, dripping scalps that was worrisome.

They rolled south, beyond the Powder River, stopping during the daylight hours only to make major repairs to the equipment. Routine chores like resetting iron tires or tightening loose wheel spokes were done at night while the mules grazed on the thick carpet of rich grass that covered the land in unbroken waves for countless miles.

"We'll be coming onto the North Platte soon," Chatham announced over the evening fire one night.

"Tomorrow," Fargo agreed.

"You seen the breaks already?"

"Uh huh." Fargo speared a chunk of fried salt pork and shoved the hot, greasy meat into his mouth.

"Either we're making better time'n I thought or you scout farther ahead than I reckoned."

"Some of each maybe."

"Be good to get to Fort Laramie, eh, boys?" Chatham wiped his mustache and beard with the back of his hand.

"Damn right, Bill." The freighter who had spoken, one of the arrogant drivers with a coiled whip always close at hand, cupped his crotch in both hands and groaned loudly. "Man gets mighty ready after so long on the road."

Chatham gave Fargo a wink, pushed a sprig of sagebrush into the fire as if he were going to relight his pipe, and then chucked the burning twig at his driver. The man ducked and laughed and thumped on his chest with a roar.

"Damn me, Bill Chatham, but I'm the rowdiest son of a bitch ever skun a mule or twisted a lion's tail."

"I believe that, Blue. Damn me if I don't." Chuckling, Chatham pushed another sprig of sage into the fire, but this time he did use it to light his pipe.

"I'm gonna turn in," Fargo said. "Long day tomorrow."

About midmorning Fargo found the remains of a Crow camp. The Crows were way the hell and gone out of their home territory, probably on their way to Fort Laramie for business. He was sure of the tribe because of the distinctive pattern they had used when they set out their tepee poles, an unusual elliptical shape quite unlike the very slight oval shape used by the Sioux and Cheyenne who might normally be expected to be seen here. The Crows were traveling peacefully, hunting as they went. He found the refuse piles where they had skinned out a small deer and several antelope. No danger from that bunch, so he left the wagons and moved on ahead after stopping only long enough to examine the camp and relieve himself.

Toward noon he thought about turning back to join Chatham and the wagons for the midday meal. He was carrying only jerky in his saddlebags and some coffee in a twist of paper. But it was a long way back to where the slow-moving wagons should be by now—farther if they'd had to stop for any repairs—and the next rise might give him a look at the North Platte and the Oregon Trail ruts that ran beside it. Something about the Oregon had never failed to send a thrill of pleasure through Skye Fargo. Or through the young and innocent man he had been before he took on the name "Fargo" and a trail of vengeance. The Oregon had been his first big trail, taken when he was young and alone and eager. The Oregon held memories for him that were untainted by disaster and pleasant to call on.

One more rise, he told himself. He'd ride ahead one more rise. If he didn't spot the trail by then, he could still turn and go back in time for supper with the wagon crews.

He nudged the Ovaro in the flanks, and the big horse bobbed his head for a moment, then eased into a fluid canter across the thick mat of buffalo grass.

Up ahead a band of a dozen or so delicate, wary antelope came bolting into view from the far side of the rise, saw the man and horse, and wheeled to race away in graceful, twenty-foot leaping strides.

Fargo smiled as he watched them go. He had no need of their meat. He wished them well.

The pinto carried him to the top of the rise, and he pulled it down to a halt so he could look for the telltale signs of bare, beaten earth amid the sea of grass, for the Oregon if he had yet reached it.

"Shit," Fargo mumbled. The Ovaro's ears flicked back and forward in silent response to the man's voice. "We got troubles, old fella. Or somebody does."

Fargo made a small adjustment with the reins, changing the pinto's direction, and the horse's head came up and his ears forward as he too saw the distant object and loped toward it.

A carriage. A damned carriage, way the hell and gone out here. Sitting alone, no draft stock anywhere in sight.

Abandoned vehicles weren't uncommon on the Oregon Trail. Even stoutly built vehicles broke down and had to be left behind. Great Conestogas were cut in two and turned into ungainly carts when axles and undercarriages broke beyond the point of repair. To find a light rig abandoned by someone damn fool enough to try the Oregon with it, well, that wouldn't be so surprising.

But Fargo thought he could also see a flutter of movement in the shade under the rig. A movement that was contrary to the little breeze blowing out of the west.

Damn!

Skye Fargo hadn't become the Trailsman by accepting things at face value. He rode closer to the carriage, then swerved wide around it.

He could see clearly now as a human figure crawled out from under the rig into the sunlight, and began waving to him. The distance was too great for him to hear, but the person was probably shouting to him also.

The figure was dressed in skirts. A woman to all appearances. Maybe it even *was* a woman, although what any female would be doing out here alone was an interesting question.

Even then Fargo didn't continue straight on to the frantically waving figure.

He completed his wide circle, making sure no enemy lay hidden in the short grass within gunshot. An Indian—or any white sensible enough to lie still and not scratch his ass all the time—could lie down on barren ground in bright, gaily colored clothing and never be noticed if he remained motionless.

Only when he was satisfied no ambush was set in the vicinity of the carriage did Fargo finally turn the pinto toward the rig.

"Thank God you found me," the woman said. She rushed forward the last few yards to meet his approach with crying and hand-grasping.

"Ma'am." Fargo touched the brim of his hat, checked the Ovaro, and stepped down from the saddle. The woman threw herself into his arms and began wetting the front of his shirt with her tears.

"It's all right now, ma'am. It's all right now." He comforted her, giving her time to adjust, then freed a hand long enough to reach for his saddlebags. "You hungry, ma'am? Thirsty? How'd you come to be here all alone?"

The sniffling died away and she gradually regained control of herself. She accepted a little jerky and a swallow of water. Then she felt up to talking.

"I'm . . . Please forgive me for breaking down like that. That isn't like me. Honestly."

"Yes, ma'am."

"My name is Roget. Mrs. Diana Ellinson Roget. I am . . . was . . ." She looked embarrassed. "I was traveling to meet my husband at Wenatchee, out in the Washington country."

"Yes, ma'am."

"I hired a guide with a party going that way. We were traveling together. Then yesterday . . . No, day before yesterday." Her face went vacant for a moment. "Good Lord, I don't remember how long it's been. Isn't that awful?"

"It's all right, ma'am. You've had a shock. Only natural for it to jumble together. You're all right now, though."

She gave him a brief look of gratitude and went on. "They said . . . they said they saw some Indians. They all became quite frightened. And my . . . my wagon broke an axle. It was the worst possible time, I know, but I hadn't planned for it to break then, you understand."

"No, ma'am." Fargo was thinking. He could start a signal fire to draw the wagons toward them, but the train was a long way back. Better to carry her with him on the pinto and get her more quickly to the comfort of company.

"Everyone was terribly frightened of the Indians."

Likely the Crows whose cold camp he had found earlier, Fargo thought. Harmless travelers, if that was the case, and no danger to anyone on the Oregon.

"They wanted to leave my wagon behind. I . . . I objected. So they took my mules and my . . . my things . . . and they just went on. Left me behind and went on as fast as they could go." She began to cry again.

Fargo calmed her again, fed her a little more jerky with apologies that he didn't have more to offer, and lifted her up behind him on the pinto.

"Won't be long now, ma'am. We'll get you back to the wagons, get a proper lunch in you, have you along to Fort Laramie almost before you know it."

"I don't know what I'd have done if you hadn't come along, Mr. Fargo."

"You'd have done just fine, ma'am." Hell, it might even have been the truth. The river was close enough that she wouldn't have thirsted too bad, and a body can go without food for a long while. She probably would have made out. Fargo didn't want her making a fuss over him for offering human kindness.

"You're safe now," he said.

The Trailsman didn't know that this was the only lie he'd ever tell her.

Happy to have been rescued by the Trailsman, Mrs. Roget loosened up; she relaxed even more once they reached the wagon train and she was surrounded by an entire group of travelers who were eager to help her.

Chatham stopped the train on the spot and ordered the crew to make camp for the night, and the hell with time lost. One of the men put up a small, seldom-used Sibley tent and showed Mrs. Roget into it. When the woman didn't come back out again in a reasonable amount of time, Fargo and Chatham went close enough to whisper an inquiry to her. The only response was a the faint sound of snoring.

"The poor woman's exhausted," Fargo said. "Don't reckon she's gotten any rest the whole time for fear of Indians or bears or who knows what. I'd say to let her sleep."

"She must be hungry too."

"Yeah, but I had a little jerky, which I gave her. It should do until she wakes up. What say you have your boys build up a good fire, and I'll go fetch us a fat antelope. Have it all ready for when she wakes."

Chatham nodded his agreement, and Fargo hefted the Sharps carbine as he turned back toward the pinto.

It was nearly dark before Mrs. Roget came out of the

tent, puffy-eyed and with her hair in disarray but looking and quite obviously feeling considerably better than she had. She had enough confidence now that she made no apologies for sleeping through the afternoon, which seemed to have done her a world of good.

"Over here, ma'am," one of Chatham's men told her. "Got everything all fixed up an' waitin' for you."

The men had set up a folding table for her use and put a camp stool beside it. Most of the rough-talking mule skinners acted as if they'd adopted the lady for a pet. One man who looked like he hadn't bathed since the start of the last decade carefully inspected each piece of cutlery before an item was deemed worthy of Mrs. Roget's use, while another two argued over which cuts of the antelope haunch would be the tastiest and most tender. Chatham winked at Fargo and let the men have their fun.

The woman was ravenously hungry after sleeping. She put away a remarkable amount of the dark, juicy meat. If the two axle wipers hadn't been able to find her the very best cuts possible, she certainly made no complaint about it.

Predictably, though, within a few minutes of eating she began to look uncomfortable. And embarrassed.

Fargo and Chatham looked politely away.

A person whose stomach has been empty for a day or better, and who then eats heavily of rich food, is quite naturally and almost necessarily going to be afflicted with sudden diarrhea. The disorder is short-lived and not at all harmful, but the victim's need for relief can be acute.

"Excuse me," Mrs. Roget muttered. She leapt off the camp stool and disappeared into the darkness with her skirts held high and a look of some distress.

Chatham winked at Fargo again and reached for his coffeecup without speaking.

The wagon crew finished off the last of the roast pronghorn. Most of the men had been holding back until their guest was done. Now they turned loose on the unexpected treat—there was no time taken for hunting while the train was in motion—and polished it off. Fargo and the wagon master did their share also.

"She's been gone a long time," Chatham said when they were working on their final cups of coffee.

"It can be like that."

"You don't think she could be having any, uh, difficulties, do you?"

"Damn few Indians or bears around that I've seen."

"I meant, uh, difficulties of a more, uh, personal nature."

"I don't know about you, Bill, but I don't figure to go out there and offer to wipe for her."

"I suppose you're right. Hard to know what's decent and proper sometimes."

Later, as the campfire was burning low, it was Fargo's turn to fidget and look off into the night. "Dammit, Bill, I'm starting to get worried."

"So'm I."

"You think we should go, well, check on her?"

"Never knew it to last this long."

"You think she might've been weaker than we thought? Might've passed out or something?"

"Kinda hard to tell about a woman. She could have some kinda female problem that we don't know about."

"Whatever it is, I'm commencing to get worried about it. She should've been back by now."

"We could take a look. Quiet like. Back off if she's all right. She wouldn't have to know we were around. Unless she needs some help, that is."

"I think you're right," Fargo agreed. "You might want to bring a lantern and matches. But we won't light it unless we have to."

"Yeah." Chatham went to the toolbox on the side of his

huge wagon and rummaged inside it for a lantern, then had to spend more time finding a tin container of coal oil so he could fill the lantern.

While Chatham was busy with that, Fargo was hoping Mrs. Roget would return on her own and prove their worries unfounded. But she didn't.

"Ready if you are, Fargo."

"Then let's go take a look."

They walked out a hundred yards in the direction the woman had taken, then stopped to listen. The only sounds were the soft soughing of the night breeze and a far-off yelping as two coyotes talked back and forth somewhere north of the distant river.

"See anything?" Chatham's voice was a whisper.

"No." Fargo shook his head.

"Too damn dark to track her."

Chatham couldn't know it, but that comment lightened the mood for the Trailsman. Fargo's reputation must have been high indeed if Bill Chatham expected him to be able to track anyone—damn near any*thing* out here on the prairie, particularly anyone as light as a thin woman. The clay earth was sunbaked as hard as pottery between the clumps of dry buffalo grass, and the only way to track anyone who moved across it on foot would be by scent.

"There's a depression over there, buffalo wallow or something. She might've gone down in there for some privacy." There certainly was nothing else within view for a person to hide behind, nothing taller than the knee-high sage until the cottonwoods and crack willow that lined the North Platte.

Fargo glanced toward the sky. The moon was rising, but it wasn't full enough to offer much light. A wisp of cloud scudded across the pale glow and passed free of it, giving them at least a little light to see by.

Fargo led the way, Chatham following close behind on

tiptoe, which was not necessarily the best way to move quietly but would do for the moment.

The bale of the lantern clacked against Chatham's thigh, and the man swore under his breath.

"Calm down, dammit," Fargo hissed, but he was feeling uncomfortable too. Nothing he could put his finger on, but he was definitely uncomfortable.

Fargo bent low and eased forward to the edge of the wallow, moving as silently as a hunting cat and not much faster.

"Oh, hell," he said in a normal voice. He straightened.

"What?" Chatham moved up beside him, still trying to be quiet.

Fargo pointed.

Mrs. Roget was there at the bottom of the wallow, all right. But the front of her dress, its skirts bunched high over her waist, was stained black in the moonlight.

"Jesus!" Chatham said.

"Light your lantern, Bill," Fargo said. "And be damn careful what you step on. We got to see what's happened here."

Chatham fumbled for a moment, and when the flame caught, the Trailsman led the wagon master down to the body of the dead woman.

"Hold the light closer. Down here." Fargo knelt on the hard, gravel-studded soil and leaned closer.

He felt embarrassed, as if Mrs. Roget would think ill of him for looking at her there, but he had no choice.

"She's been raped."

"I see it." Chatham's voice was rasping, harsh.

In addition to the dark stains of drying blood on the bunched-up dress and on Mrs. Roget's lower belly, there were pale, slick-shiny stains on the insides of her thighs and matted into her pubic hair, sparce, and for the most part gray. The woman had been aging. No young beauty.

Whoever killed her hadn't cared about that. He raped her first, then knifed her repeatedly in the chest and upper abdomen. She was raped before she was stabbed; the blood on her stomach hadn't been smeared by the rapist's belly.

Fargo reached down to touch the blood—barely tacky, well along toward being dry—and then the crusty semen left behind by the unknown man, completely dry already. She was probably dead before they had begun to worry about her absence from the camp. Fargo said so.

"Jesus!" Chatham said again but softly—as a prayer, not an epithet. The wagon master bent his head and crossed himself quickly, the action of a man trying to ward evil away. He looked at Fargo. "Indians."

The Trailsman shook his head. "Huh uh. White man."

"That can't be, Fargo."

"Yeah. But it was." He pulled the hem of the dead woman's dress down to cover her nakedness, then motioned toward her throat. "That necklace. The brooch pinned on her dress there. If it'd been an Indian, he would've taken those for sure. Carry them home and give them to the missus after he'd done with his raping. White man, now, particularly one traveling right along with us, he wouldn't want to carry off anything that could be used to identify him as the rapist."

To Fargo, perhaps to Chatham as well, the rape was more offensive than the murder. This was hard country. People died in it every day and only the lucky ones were buried. Murder was almost commonplace. But there were some things that simply were not done. Even a whore had the right of refusal. To violate a decent woman like Mrs. Roget was unthinkable.

Chatham's jaw hardened. "One of my own men . . . ?"

"You know of any other white men in the neighborhood?"

Chatham looked like he wanted to be sick. Fargo didn't blame him.

"We have to find him, Fargo. We have to."

"We will," Fargo promised, his voice as cold as the steely glitter in his lake-blue eyes. That lake had frozen over, and for some son of a bitch it was going to be a long, hard winter before the thaw set in. "We will."

The men of the train were as shocked and angry as Bill Chatham had been. They growled obscenely and stood apart from one another, friendships abandoned for the moment and suspicions on a hair-trigger edge.

"First things first," Fargo said, assuming command of the group by habit rather than by conscious decision. "You and you and you, go bring the lady's body in. We won't wash her. Wouldn't be decent for strangers to see her that way. But we want to get her buried quick as possible. While they're bringing her in, the rest of you break out some picks and start a grave. Whoever isn't busy digging can carry in whatever rocks or stones you can find. We don't want her dug up and the coyotes after her once we've gone."

The men went in grim silence to the tasks. In less than an hour the willing hands had forced a hole in the hard earth, and the body was ready for burial. One of the axle wipers who had argued about the cut of meat Mrs. Roget should have now insisted on contributing his best blanket to serve as her coffin and her shroud. Chatham offered a brief service while the men stood bareheaded and silent. The lonely grave was quickly covered, unmarked save for the rocks that covered it. Any more would have invited disturbance by passing Indians, who would have wanted the jewelry buried with Mrs. Roget.

"Now," Fargo said when the chore was done. "Now we find out who else dies tonight."

Even Chatham looked startled.

"Is everyone of your party here, Mr. Chatham?" the Trailsman asked.

The train master stabbed a forefinger at each man in turn, mentally counting them off one by one, this mule skinner, that wiper, that packer. "Almost," he said finally. "Tom Burnett's out with the stock."

"Call him in, if you please. We'll all get this business over and done with."

Chatham nodded and motioned for one of the men to go bring the missing nightherder in.

Fargo's expression was blank. It might have been carved from slate. He didn't speak again until every member of the train crew was assembled. Then he built the campfire into a bright, roaring tower that cast its flickering light around the full circle of the company.

"One of you men raped and murdered Mrs. Roget," he said. "The others of you don't deserve the suspicion that man put you under. And that man, whichever one of you it is, doesn't deserve to live to see the sunrise."

Fargo looked slowly around the circle, his eyes meeting those of each and every other man in the group. Unhurried. Coldly certain.

"Whoever did that foul piece of work tonight will also die this night."

A low, ugly murmur of agreement fluttered through the silence around the crackling campfire.

"Whoever killed that lady left his stinking seed on her body. The son of a bitch also left it on himself. He marked himself with it, and now it will mark him the rest of us to find. One by one, boys, I want each of you around the circle to open your flies. Let everybody see. I'll be the first."

Fargo took a step forward and set the example. He exposed himself, looking not down toward his own body but boldly into the eyes of every other man in the circle of light.

He had thought that some of the more timid or shy of the men might balk at the unusual request, but the mood was quickly set by a burly skinner who stepped forward. "I'm next, by God," the man declared. "An' then I want a piece o' the son of a cowardly bitch what done this." He opened his fly.

The other men hurried to join him.

Most of the other men—not by any means all of them.

It was this that the Trailsman was counting on. By now hours had passed since the lady died. More than enough time for any obvious traces of the deed to dry or be wiped away.

Fargo was counting on the bastard's own guilt, and the deadly fury of the fellow's own companions, to unnerve him and make him refuse to participate in what was in truth no more than a childish ritual of displayed innocence.

The man known as Blue held back. Fargo saw beads of sweat break out on Blue's forehead, and he began to squirm like he had body lice.

Fargo moved around the circle until he was facing Blue across the leaping flames of the campfire. He stared at Blue, eyes narrowed and lips drawn tight in silent accusation.

Blue blanched pale and raised a trembling hand to his throat. He seemed to be having difficulty swallowing. He took one tottering, uncertain step backward, and then another. He moved awkwardly, stiff-legged. Fargo stared into his eyes.

With a cry of sudden panic, Blue broke. He spun on his heel and ran shrieking into the darkness—away from the accusing light of the fire, away from the men who until this moment had been his friends and fellow travelers. He ran with the speed of terror.

But there was no way he could run quickly enough, no chance he could run far enough.

The men who until this moment had been Blue's friends whirled and charged after him, yelping and yipping like a pack of hounds on a scent.

Few of the men were armed. At least not with guns. All carried knives. Many held their bullwhacker whips coiled in their fists.

They raced off into the night with screams of raw, animal fury tearing from their throats.

Fargo stood where he was. Let the man's companions take their revenge for the cloud Blue had placed over each of them. There was no need for the Trailsman on this ugly chase.

He looked across the fire to where Bill Chatham also stood. Chatham crossed himself, and his lips moved wordlessly. But he looked disinclined to interfere.

From somewhere out in the darkness there was the loud, snapping report of a bullwhip cracking. Then a scream of pain and terror.

More whips popped and more yet as the freighters surrounded their prey and cut him to pieces inch by shrieking inch.

Fargo and Chatham could hear well enough; they didn't need to see.

Chatham stood where he was, listening. Then after a moment, while the sounds from the night continued, he shuddered once and turned away. "Coffee?"

"Sure," Fargo said. "Why not?"

6

The Trailsman left Bill Chatham and his freighters at Fort Laramie on the great, empty grass that seemed to cover half the continent. Chatham and his men alike were subdued, the normal ebullience of an arrival left behind with the unburied body of the man named Blue.

"You sure you wouldn't want to wait and come south with us?" Chatham offered. "We might hold you up only a matter of days."

"No, but I thank you for the offer." The wagons would be traveling south to deliver the stamp mill to its new owner. The Colorado camps, Fargo had heard, were threatening to compete even with the mighty Comstock in richness and impact.

"Go ahead then," Chatham said, "and good fortune go with you."

"Will you . . . ?"

"Aye, I'll make a report to the authorities here. And get off a letter to Mr. Roget at Wenatchee. The man deserves to know. Some of it anyway."

Fargo shook hands with Chatham and his crew. They were good men, solid, the kind who could come into an empty land and make it a decent place to live. Good men to ride with.

Fargo forked the sturdy Ovaro and splashed across the North Platte, leaving the Oregon Trail now and moving straight south.

This was still Sioux country. But soon he would be entering territory used mostly by the Arapaho. He expected no trouble. On the other hand, he was ready for trouble if it chose to come his way. That was part of the wariness that had become a part of the Trailsman's daily life, the price he had to pay for the right to remain alive.

Traveling alone through a country so vast and empty would have made most men timid. Even the vaunted, adventurous mountain men of a generation earlier preferred to cross this land in brigades of their own kind. But Skye Fargo was no ordinary man. He had been forged and tempered in the fire of burning gunpowder until only the solid steel was left. Riding alone held no terrors for him.

No trailblazing was necessary here. There was a trail of sorts to follow, leading to the booming camps where gold had been found. He pushed the Ovaro as hard as common sense allowed, each day covering twice the distance that the wagons could have managed. Finally, he reached the twin towns of Cherry Creek and Auraria, lately becoming known under the single name of Denver.

A few men still tried to scrape out a living from placer claims in the gravel of Cherry Creek where the gold rush had been started. But Denver was quickly becoming a place of commerce where mining supplies could be had at the end of the freight roads coming out from Kansas and where the miners from the mountains could spend the wages they had earned deep under the ground.

Fargo had been there before, but Denver had grown in the time he had been away. Probably five, six thousand residents now, and the boom still on. Of course if the mountain camps played out and exhausted their lodes, Denver too might very well cease to exist almost over-night, its population packing up and moving on to the next strike. It happened that way often, and a man never knew if the town where he found rest tonight would even exist tomorrow.

The Trailsman stopped in Denver only long enough to restock his provisions and to ask the Overland Express agent about a young, redhaired woman who might have arrived here December last.

"Mister, you got to be kidding me. December? A passenger? Man, I don't think I could remember the people that worked for me that long ago. People are coming through here all the time. I don't any sooner get a fella hired than he's got the gold fever and gone traipsing upriver thinking he'll be rich tomorrow." The agent shook his head in exasperation. "December?" He shook his head again.

Fargo thanked the man and reclaimed the pinto from the livery where the animal had been getting much-deserved rest and grain.

The road along the South Platte leading into the mountains was clearly marked, its ruts worn deep by the iron-rimmed wheels of the great wagons that carried material up into the camps, then turned and brought back mineral concentrates for smelting into valuable metals.

The stamp mills that accompanied the mines could only do as much of the recovery process, breaking down raw ore, discarding so much waste rock as possible, and returning a charcoal-colored, glittering concentrate heavy with gold and silver and base metals like zinc and lead and copper. Refining the concentrates into recognizable, nearly pure elements had to be done in huge volume, and Denver supplied the service.

The South Platte, a flat and ugly excuse for a river down

on the prairie, grew livelier close to its origins, racing its way through slender gorges and leaping jagged boulders high above the grassy plains.

The Ovaro stepped delicately across bare, slick rock next to the river as the road continued its climb. The broad, empty reaches of grass and sky had been left behind. Now the horizon might be no more than a few yards distant. Fargo rode surrounded by towers of gray, bare rock that loomed above the Ovaro for impossible distances, up and up until they touched the very clouds.

Even the foliage changed here, the rich buffalo grass giving way to gravel and rock and a few dry sprigs of bunchgrass. The cottonwoods and crack willow and wild plum couldn't survive here. Instead, there were only a few spruce and aspen. And not many of those could find a foothold on the scanty soil of the high country.

It was damned different here. Fargo could feel it inside his own chest, the air offering little sustenance for a man's lungs, any vigorous exertion pulling at him, draining him without warning. It was a thing to remember.

He stopped first at Georgetown, a tiny community as gray as the mountain walls that surrounded it, with not a tree in sight. The few that had grown nearby had long since been stripped away and used for shaft timbers. Now even their stumps were being put to use. Fargo saw men grubbing stumps and roots out of the ground and loading them into wagons, bits of wood useless for shoring but valued as fuel in a wood-hungry mining camp.

Here there wouldn't have been much traffic—certainly not many women—passing through. He very well might be able to find Margaret Fitzroy, or Anne Roy if she preferred, and give her the chance Fargo would never have: the chance to once again see her father.

He felt good about that as he reined the Ovaro to a stop in front of Georgetown's one and only livery stable.

"You've earned your keep for this night," Fargo muttered to the horse while he stripped off his saddle and gear and got out his dandybrush. "But it looks like you'll have to spend it in the company of mules and burros."

Work animals seemed to be the ruling class of livestock here, mules to draw the heavy wagons up from Denver, burros to draw the ore carts deep underground.

With luck, Fargo thought as he inspected the pinto's feet, that reunion of the Fitzroys might be little more than a telegraph wire away.

"Yes. Oh, my, yes." The clerk at the stage company's office blushed. "Yes, I do recall the young lady." Fondly, Fargo guessed, and very well indeed to have such a reaction all these months later. The fellow was almost certainly blushing not because of things he had done but because of the things he had thought about doing. The man had a very-married look about him.

"She did come here, then?"

The clerk nodded. "Just as you said. Around the beginning of the year. I couldn't say if it was December, though. Might have been January. Is that important?"

Fargo shook his head. He was sure it wasn't. Margaret Fitzroy would have arrived in Denver the second week of December, so she must have gotten to Georgetown shortly thereafter. Exactly when made no difference. So long as she was here. . . . Or was she? She could have moved on already.

Fargo asked, and again the shy clerk blushed. "I am quite sure she must still be here. I would certainly remember if she took a coach out again."

"You don't happen to know where she is living, where she might work?"

The man shook his head. "That is strange when you think about it. I haven't seen her since she arrived."

Only odd, Fargo realized, if the stage agent spent much time in town. More likely he spent his working hours here in this cramped little office and then went straight home to his wife at night.

Fargo thanked him and went back out into the bright heat of the high-country sunshine. Even the sun itself seemed to have an extra bite in it at this elevation, although the temperatures were pleasant enough. At night it probably became quite cool, even in the summer.

There weren't so very many places in Georgetown where a respectable young lady might stay. Fargo tried the most obvious of them first: three transient hotels and a good many boardinghouses, ranging from private homes, where a few square feet of surplus space could be let out, to the multistoried commercial outfits, where the hard-rock miners could bunk and eat for a fixed weekly rate.

Fargo inquired first at the nicest of the hotels. No single ladies were registered for long-term residence. Since Fitzroy was paying the bills this trip, Fargo registered as a guest himself and then went along down the principal street to ask about Margaret at the other hotels.

He had been, he realized, assuming that Fitzroy's daughter would be traveling and living well. But that could well be a false assumption. Fitzroy himself had said he hadn't been a man of wealth when he last saw his daughter. He had left his family in search of the wealth that later came to him. And Donald Powell's prospects mustn't have been all that grand or the man wouldn't have ended as a spurious mining engineer in a backwater like Virginia City. Margaret, or Anne if she preferred, was more likely living in modest circumstances. Fargo's assumptions had been natural enough, taken from her father, but they were very likely false.

Anticipation, the expected pleasure of being able to give

these two their reunion, was clouding his judgment. That was something the Trailsman couldn't allow himself.

"No," the man running the Washingtonian said. "I have a pair of young ladies staying here, but neither is named Roy or Fitzroy."

"Either of them have red hair?" Fargo asked. There was a possibility that she might have changed her name again. Hell, come to think of it, she might have married since she came here. Everyone certainly talked up her looks. And a pretty young woman who wanted to marry could damn sure find the opportunity for it in a mining camp five minutes after making up her mind that she wanted to take herself a husband. Most any eligible male she might pass on the street. Decent young women, especially attractive ones, were almighty rare in a mining town.

"Nope," the clerk said. He gave Fargo a searching look. Questions about single women wouldn't necessarily be well received, or legitimately offered, and this man's suspicions seemed to have been aroused.

"Reckon neither of them is the lady I'm looking for, then," Fargo said politely.

"Why you askin', mister?"

"Miss Fitzroy's father is trying to locate her," Fargo explained. There was no reason to hide that fact, and if the word got around town, it just might reach Margaret and make his search all the shorter.

The clerk grunted, still apparently skeptical but satisfied for the moment. "All right, then."

Fargo thanked the man and went on. He checked the last hotel with no better results and then broke off the search for the moment. He was dry and hungry, and he was beginning to suspect he wouldn't find the girl easily.

After supper he inquired at the businesses up and down the length of the main street.

Margaret worked at none of them.

More curiously, none of the sales clerks and proprietors he talked with remembered having done business with her.

Dammit, she was here in Georgetown. He'd established that, hadn't he? So she had to be living someplace, working someplace, buying her food and clothing at one of the local shops.

This wasn't adding up, Fargo thought with frustration.

Something wasn't ringing true.

How in hell could a single woman—a good-looking and memorable single woman at that—disappear in a gold camp the size of Georgetown?

Couldn't be done. That was the only answer. It just couldn't be done.

Yet, if the Trailsman was to believe what everyone was telling him here, it had happened.

One thing he could count on: he wasn't being tricked. An entire town couldn't get together and stick with a lie. Not everybody in it. A few people, sure, if they had a good reason for it. But not the whole damn camp. Huh uh.

No, the odds were that the people he was talking to were telling him the truth the way they saw it. The stage agent remembered her getting here. No one remembered seeing her since.

How could that be?

There were possibilities, of course, however remote they might be. The girl could have been kidnapped, even murdered. If that was so . . .

Fargo went cold just thinking about it.

If Fitzroy's dream of a reunion with his child had been crushed the same way Fargo's family had been destroyed . . .

The Trailsman's expression went coldly grim and his eyes began to take on the hard glitter of frozen lake water. A man passing on the street paled and hurried to get out of Fargo's way, stammering an apology even though he had

97

done nothing to apologize for. Fargo hadn't been paying any attention to him at all. And did not now. The Trailsman's thoughts at the moment were far away and not at all pleasant.

For the next two days Fargo talked with damned near everyone in the camp who might have noticed a single woman living there, and he still had no further information about Margaret Anne. It was as maddening as it was illogical.

He tugged his hat lower over his eyes and headed for the restaurant where he'd been taking his meals. It was evening, and up and down the main street the shops were beginning to close and people streamed out of them toward their homes. There was no pretty redhead among them, though. He knew that all too well. The hell with it. Time to get some supper. Then look for the girl some more. Although where? He shook his head impatiently. He had already as good as exhausted the possibilities here with no success whatsoever. Dammit.

"Mr. Fargo, wait a moment please."

Fargo turned. The clerk from the stage office was hurrying along the sidewalk toward him. "Yes?"

"Are you still looking for that, um, young woman?" He flushed slightly.

"I sure as hell am," Fargo conceded.

"Then I have good news for you," the clerk said, breathless.

Fargo couldn't be sure if the fellow's difficulty came from his excitement about Margaret Anne or if it were simply because he'd had to walk so fast to catch up with the long-legged strides of the Trailsman.

"She came by the stage office again this afternoon," the clerk said in a rush of words. "This very afternoon." He was smiling.

All the frustration and disappointment fell away, and

Fargo felt as excited and eager now as the clerk. That reunion was going to happen. Fargo swore that it was. "Where is she now? Here in Georgetown? Where? Do you know, man?"

"Slow down, Mr. Fargo. Please." The man was out of breath but grinning with the pleasure he shared with Skye Fargo.

"I'm sorry. Now tell me."

"Of course. Of course. Just let me get my breath a moment."

Fargo waited impatiently while the little clerk bent forward from the waist and gulped in several quick drafts of the clear mountain air, then straightened, still grinning hugely.

"She was at the stage office today, just like I said. She was buying a ticket, you see. But I recognized her immediately. Just as I remembered. Dear me, such a lovely young woman, you see."

"But . . ."

"I know what you intend to ask, Mr. Fargo. Yes, indeed I did tell her that you were inquiring about her. Indeed, I did, sir. But she was in a great hurry. She bought a ticket on the evening coach to Central City. She was in quite a rush." The man lowered his voice and looked around to make sure they were not overheard.

"She asked me not to tell anyone that she was leaving or where she was going, you see. Probably avoiding some persistent young man would be my guess. A rejected suitor, someone like that. There were others waiting in line for tickets. I couldn't take the time to explain to her. And of course, I shouldn't tell anyone, wouldn't tell anyone but you, Mr. Fargo. But I realize you're only trying to be helpful, find her for her father and all that. So I don't feel it would be breaking her confidence to tell you this, you see."

"Of course." Fargo nodded.

"I wanted to rush out and find you immediately, but I had those other customers, and the driver was already making up the team—she had come in at quite the last possible moment to catch the stage, you see—and so I simply hadn't the time to find you before she left. But now you know where to find her, you see. So I thought—"

"You did just fine," Fargo interrupted. "You've been a great help, and I know she'll thank you, too. Her father sure will."

The stage-line clerk beamed with pleasure. "I'm so glad you aren't angry with me."

Fargo suspected that people were often angry with the meek little man. "She's already left, though?"

"Oh, yes. Bought her ticket and climbed right onto the coach, even before the team was hitched. She seemed most anxious to avoid whoever it is who was pestering her. She was wearing a hat to cover her hair and a veil over her face. But I recognized her at once. One simply doesn't forget a young woman so attractive as that, you see."

"Of course," Fargo said.

The clerk was blushing again. Fargo guessed that the man's wife was going to be busy this night.

"Could I buy you a drink?" Fargo offered. He wanted to thank the fellow for the help he had given.

"A drink? Dear me, no. I'm temperance, you know. No spirits, no tobacco. Wouldn't touch them." He sounded a bit wistful, making his declaration; likely that temperance business was the idea of the missus and not the supposed head of the family.

"If you're sure," Fargo said.

"Yes, quite, but it is nice of you to offer."

"And she was going to Central City, you say."

"Yes, indeed." The man pulled a watch from his vest

pocket and checked the time. "They should be nearly there by now. I came to find you the instant I could get away."

Fargo thanked the man again, pleased now that the fellow had declined a time-consuming drink, and turned toward the livery where the Ovaro stabled. The road was well-enough-marked and the moon rose early. He could be in Central City before midnight.

"Good luck," the clerk called to Fargo's retreating back.

7

Central City was a blaze of lights when Fargo rode in. The town was the territorial capital and a hotbed of politics and mining. Despite that dignified veneer, though, the place appeared to be just a larger and busier version of a mining camp, its saloons and brothels active day and night. The only difference seemed to be that one was as likely to see broadcloth suits here as mud-crusted coveralls.

Fargo found a place to stable the Ovaro and temporarily store his saddlebags and began looking for Margaret Fitzroy even before he took the time to check into a hotel.

The stage-company office was his logical first stop, but while most of Central City was still roaringly busy at this late hour, the stage station was closed and dark behind a heavy padlock on the front door.

Fargo mumbled a few curses under his breath and began looking around for any nearby loafers who might have seen the recent stage from Georgetown unload.

There was no one in sight. This end of the street was unlighted and virtually empty of traffic, although a few blocks away he could see the glare of bright lamps and hear the whooping of gamblers trying their luck at the faro tables and the wheels of fortune.

Fargo stifled a yawn and turned toward the bright lights. Maybe at one of the hotels . . .

A rustle of movement off to his right caught his attention. It was the faintest of sounds, a whisper of cloth against cloth. Anyone less actuely attuned to his surroundings would certainly have missed it, but the Trailsman's attentions were seldom dull. He couldn't afford for them to be. Not that he was expecting trouble here in Central City, but the habits of caution were strong.

He turned, intending to find the man and ask about Margaret.

As soon as Fargo altered his course and turned back toward the sound, he heard a sudden intake of breath, a soft sound of surprise.

And immediately thereafter he heard the oily, metallic *clack-clack* of a weapon's hammer sear being drawn across the trigger stop.

Fargo's reaction was instant and instinctive. He dropped into a crouch and threw himself sideways into a shoulder roll, his hand already clawing for the Colt at his belt.

The peaceful quiet of the night was blown apart by a spout of yellow flame and a deafening roar as a shotgun exploded from the shadows not twenty paces distant, its charge of heavy shot sizzling through the air where a moment before Fargo's torso had been. If he hadn't heard that subtle sound, if he hadn't leapt aside . . .

The Trailsman's Colt spat in instant response, its sleek muzzle searching the shadows and aiming just to the right of where the shotgun flame had been.

The light of the first muzzle flash had barely had time to die away before Fargo's smaller flame split the night.

The Army Colt bucked in the Trailsman's hand and he fired again and rolled away, changing position before the unseen ambusher could have time to react.

Fargo heard the dull, beef-and-cleaver slap of lead striking flesh and heard a grunt of pain.

At least one of his shots had found its mark.

The gunman groaned aloud, and Fargo heard the clatter of a weapon falling to the hard earth.

Fargo jumped to his feet, Colt leveled and ready, but he could see nothing for the moment. The bright flame of the muzzle flashes had disrupted his night vision.

There was a sound of retreating footsteps from behind the corner of the closed and darkened stage station. The ambusher was getting away.

Fargo raced forward, the cocked and lethal Colt leading the way. His right shin crashed painfully into some obstruction low to the ground and he felt himself falling. He tucked his shoulder low and rolled, ending up sprawled awkwardly against a tight bale of grass hay.

Quickly he came to his feet again. But by then it was already too late. Whoever the gunman was, whatever he had been doing there, he was gone now, disappeared into an alley and into the night.

Fargo stopped and listened, but he could hear nothing now. No sound of running feet. Nothing but a stir of activity behind him as lamps were lighted behind nearby windows and men began to move with slow, tentative inquiry into the street.

Fargo found a match in his pocket and lighted it. The ambusher was gone now and the townspeople of Central City were coming out to investigate the disturbance. The Trailsman had no intention of being mistaken for a lurking assassin himself. Being shot by mistake by some self-righteous citizen would be a bit of a bitch.

He pulled a handful of hay from the bale by his feet, twisted it into a makeshift torch, and lighted it.

The shotgun the gunman had dropped was there on the ground. The man had been carrying a stubby, sawed-off

single-barrel percussion gun. He hadn't had a second barrel to fire at the Trailsman. Not that Fargo was complaining.

There were also a few splatters of fresh blood gleaming
dark and shiny in the light of the makeshift torch. So the
man was wounded, whoever he was. The twist of burning
hay grew short. Fargo dropped it and ground the remains
of it under his boot as the first curious citizen arrived,
quickly followed by others, now that one had been bold
enough to prove it was safe for the rest of them.

"What the hell's going on here?" someone demanded.

Fargo shrugged. "Damned if I know, neighbor." He
waited for the rest of the bolder local men. He explained
what had happened.

Someone produced a lantern and lighted it. The shotgun
lay in the dirt where it had fallen, telltale drops of blood
near it.

"You're lucky, mister. Somebody sure as shit has it in
for you."

"Couldn't have been for me," Fargo said, feeling tired
all of a sudden. "Mistaken identity is all I can figure,
mister. I just now got into town and don't know a soul
here. Sure as hell don't have any enemies that I'd know
of."

"Likely just a damn sneak thief, then," a man specu-
lated aloud. "It happens. Good town, but you can't keep
all the riffraff out."

Fargo didn't bother to contradict the speaker, but a
sneak thief wasn't very damned likely to use a shotgun.
Shotguns tend to be a touch on the noisy side. "Whatever
you say," Fargo muttered.

A Central City police officer in a blue coat and incon-
gruous plaid trousers reached the group and in a loud voice
demanded order from the already quiet and orderly bunch of
men. Fargo had to explain the incident all over again for
the officer's benefit.

The officer heard him out, then said, "No harm done, the way I see it. You can all go back to your beds now." He glared at the men who had gathered around and then glared harder at the Trailsman. "An' you watch yourself, mister. We don't take to this kinda thing here."

Fargo gave the man a look of disgust. The fool apparently had difficulty remembering who was the victim here and who the would-be assassin.

"Yeah," Fargo said, tired now and wanting a drink and some sleep. "Yeah, I'll try to do that."

The policeman grunted something that Fargo couldn't hear—and likely it was just as well that he couldn't—picked up the shotgun and stalked off into the night.

"Thanks a hell of a lot," Fargo said softly as the last of the curious returned to their homes and the policeman turned a corner out of sight.

Fargo ate an early breakfast the next morning. He wanted to be at the stage office when it opened so he could talk to the people there and try to get a line on Margaret Anne. She was only a few hours ahead of him, but he'd been able to learn nothing last night.

He broke a biscuit in half, sopped it in the rich red-eye gravy on his plate, and chewed the result with pleasure. At least breakfast was going right.

The thin, early-morning light falling across his table was blocked by shadow, and Fargo looked up to see a huge, middle-aged man looming over him. The man was big, not with fat but with solid muscle. His suit bulged at the shoulders and arms, barely able to contain the bulk of the man. The newcomer was probably in his fifties, balding, but he looked fit enough to take on half a dozen men half his age and whip them all. He wore a highly polished brass star on the lapel of his coat.

"Something I can do for you?" Fargo asked.

The man helped himself to a seat across the table from Fargo without waiting for an invitation. He waved a hand, and the waiter appeared almost at once with a cup of coffee.

"I asked was there something I could do for you," Fargo said. There was something about this big man that Fargo didn't like. And the fellow had yet to say a word.

The officer took his time about answering. He gave a shot at staring the Trailsman down. When that failed to work, he reached into his pocket and brought out a fat, expensive-looking cigar that he trimmed and lighted before he finally bothered to speak.

"More like something I can do for you," the big man said.

"Really?"

"I'm Big Dan Finnerty." He said it like that was supposed to mean something, even to total strangers.

Finnerty waited for a reaction. But even if Fargo had known who the hell Big Dan Finnerty was, Big Dan would have had a long, cold wait for any response from the Trailsman.

"I'm the chief of police here," Finnerty finally announced, giving up on the silent intimidation.

"So?"

"You'd be the drifter that was involved in the gunfight last night," Finnerty said.

"That's not exactly the way I'd have put it, but it's true enough that somebody took a shot at me last night. I shot back. If there's supposed to be something wrong with that around here, well, I expect you'd better explain it to me."

Finnerty grunted. "That's your story, huh?"

"That's right," Fargo said agreeably, refusing to be intimidated by the manner of the police chief. "That is my story."

"Could be it isn't the whole story."

"No doubt. The other guy has a story to tell too. I hope you can find him and ask what it is." Fargo sopped the other half of his biscuit in the red-eye and ignored Finnerty while he enjoyed the flavor of it.

"Something you'd best know about this town, mister," Finnerty said in a low voice.

"And you're going to tell me what it is, right?"

"Damn right I am, mister. I'm going to tell you that we don't take kindly to gunfights in Central City. We run us a nice little town here. Quiet. We like for it to stay that way."

"Well, Chief, I'm all for peace and quiet. You could say that I'm extra partial to both. So if you can run your town so that people aren't shooting at me out of the dark, I'll just be real tickled to not touch my gun again for as long as I'm here. And as much longer as I can manage, too. I got no beef with anybody in this town. Including you, far as I know." Fargo took a swallow of coffee and gave Finnerty a long, searching look over the rim of his cup. "Or am I mistaken about that?"

The police chief met Fargo's gaze for only a matter of seconds. Then the big man's eyes dropped away toward the ash on the end of his cigar. "No," he said weakly. "No mistake."

"Good," Fargo declared. "Then we understand each other. I came here peaceful and friendly. I intend to stay that way just as long as people let me."

"Yeah . . . well . . . all right, then."

"It was nice of you to stop by," Fargo said. "And by the way, you didn't ask, but I'm just fine. Wasn't hurt a bit by that fella with the shotgun."

"Don't get smart-ass with me, mister," Finnerty snapped. "I read the report my officer turned in last night. I knew you weren't hit. I also know that the other fellow was and that the only account of it is what you told my officer. So don't play lily-white with me. If I find out anything different from what you reported last night, mister, I'll have your ass behind bars so deep and so long that you'll forget what sunshine looks like. Now do we understand each other?"

Fargo smiled at him. "We understand each other right well, Chief."

But that was true only to a degree.

Fargo understood well enough that he was under suspicion here. But why? Suspected of what? And in particular, why this interest by the chief himself?

So far the Trailsman had done nothing more suspicious than to ride into town and find a bed for the night. So why this interest in him now?

There wasn't any place in the country where a man was expected to let other people shoot at him, so that really shouldn't have anything to do with it.

Fargo shook his head as he watched the police chief leave, his coffee untouched. Damned odd, Fargo thought. Damned odd.

He finished his breakfast and headed to the stage office as he'd intended. The line was short and he was soon able to ask his questions.

"Nope," the clerk said without hesitation, and without looking Fargo in the eyes, the Trailsman noticed. The fellow was intent on a stack of papers on the counter that separated them. He was moving the papers into piles and then putting them together again, a make-work shuffling with no obvious purpose. Fargo guessed there was no purpose save to keep the man from having to look at him. "No such passenger on last night's inbound from Georgetown."

"You're sure about that," Fargo said.

"Said I was, didn't I? I'm sure."

"And no one could have gotten off that coach without you seeing them?"

"Nobody," the stage clerk said firmly. "I was here to greet the coach. Seen the passengers off my own self. Helped Charlie unhitch and bed the team 'cause old Harry, damn rummy, he got drunk again an' didn't show up to work after his dinner break. No such woman as you're looking for on that coach last night."

The clerk still hadn't once met Fargo's penetrating gaze. Which was just as well. He looked unhappy enough as it was. He would've been all the more uncomfortable if he'd seen the accusation in Fargo's eyes.

"Thanks," Fargo said.

He turned and left the stage-company office, not believing a word the man had said but having no choice about it short of grabbing the clerk by the throat and choking the truth out of him. After the visit from Chief Finnerty, that didn't seem like much of a good idea. Not quite yet anyway.

That was interesting, Fargo thought as he walked slowly back toward the center of town. This guy claimed that Margaret Anne hadn't been on the night coach. Fargo knew she had been on it, at least when it left Georgetown. As far as he knew, there were no scheduled stops in between.

It was remotely possible, of course, that she might have gotten off somewhere along the route, or chosen to leave the rig as it approached Central City.

But that was damned unlikely, in particular seeing the way that stage clerk refused to look at him.

The man acted as if he was expecting Fargo's visit, expecting to be questioned about that particular passenger, and as if he'd been damn well told to deny that Margaret Anne had been aboard the coach.

Why that should be was beyond Fargo's knowledge at

the moment. It was enough right now that the clerk's denials strengthened Fargo's belief that Margaret Anne was indeed here in Central City. Just as she had indeed been somewhere in Georgetown while he was there looking for her.

But, dammit, why would she, or anyone, be deliberately trying to keep him from finding her?

He'd made it clear enough that he meant her no harm, that he was only trying to find her for her father's sake.

Yet someone knew he was looking for her. And that someone was deliberately trying to keep him from reaching her.

Fargo's stride faltered for a moment as a thought struck him: if someone was trying to keep him from finding Margaret Anne, was it also possible that there had been a connection between that interference and the shotgun attack last night?

It certainly made no sense to think that the unprovoked attack was that of a casual thief. Not when the attacker had struck with the thunder and lightning of a sawed-off scattergun.

So he had to consider it at least possible that there was a connection. First the ambusher. Now the blatant lies from that sleeve-gartered clerk back there.

Hell, maybe there was even some connection between this unknown party's interest in keeping him away from Margaret Anne and that otherwise inexplicable visit from Big Dan Finnerty.

Some connection perhaps. But what? What possible reason could anyone have for keeping him away from a girl whose father yearned to see her again?

This seemingly innocent and delightful job was becoming stranger by the hour.

Unconsciously Fargo's fingertips stroked the grips of his

Colt and his eyes cut sideways around him, surveying the other people he could see on the streets of Central City.

Wagon traffic was heavy in the streets, huge, cumbersome rigs hauling supplies to the many stores; still-larger rigs hauling shiny, charcoal-colored concentrates away from the stamp mills en route to the smelters down on the flatlands; horsemen and pedestrians hurrying back and forth on their own business.

Fargo's lips twisted in bitter amusement as he saw across the street and half a block behind him the conspicuous blue coat of a local copper-button. One of Big Dan's boys, no doubt told to keep an eye on the troublemaker new in town.

"Well, I'll be a son of a bitch," Fargo mused under his breath. It seemed he was becoming an almighty interesting fellow, just by walking the streets.

To test his theory that he was being followed by the cop, he continued his pace to the next street corner, turned into the side street, and a few yards beyond found an alley to duck into. He leaned against the back wall of a haberdasher's shop with his arms folded and waited. Within seconds he could hear the quick tread of someone turning into the street, pausing for only a moment when there was no receding back in sight, and then hurrying on in an attempt to catch up.

The policeman scurried past the mouth of the alley where the Trailsman was waiting.

"Looking for someone?" Fargo asked mildly.

The cop nearly jumped out of his skin. He whirled and blinked a guilty look toward Fargo. "No. Uh . . . no," he said clumsily.

"If you say so." Fargo smiled at him. "Care to walk along with me?"

"No. Of course not."

Fargo shrugged. "Whatever you say." He gave the

policeman another easy smile and left the alley, ambling down the side street as if he hadn't a care in the world.

The cop stood indecisively behind him for a moment, then with a scowl turned and went the other way.

Fargo grinned to himself. So the guy had been told he wasn't supposed to be seen. If they expected to get away with that, they were going to have to do a damn sight better job of it than assigning uniformed coppers to the chore.

And someone brighter than that poor son of a bitch besides. The fellow'd acted as if he'd been caught with his hand in the candy jar.

Fargo wandered on, seemingly paying no attention to anything but in fact keenly aware of everything and everyone around him. In particular back behind him where he'd last seen that copper. He had no particular destination in mind, so he wound a circuitous path through the streets of the busy town and eventually found himself approaching the cat-house district where the red-globed lanterns were burning even at this early hour.

Never a rest for the wicked, Fargo mused.

He found a bench in front of a disreputable-looking saloon and settled on it, intending to wait a little while and see if that copper or one of his friends was still sneaking along behind.

"Skye. Skye Fargo! Yoohoo. Up here."

The happy yelling was coming from a second-floor window across the street. It took Fargo a moment to spot the woman who was shouting to him and several more moments to recognize her. She was leaning out the window as far as she could manage without falling to the street below, her hair a long, dark spill and her clothing acceptable for public display only at this end of town, wearing nothing but a fetchingly flimsy chemise that couldn't completely contain a remarkably abundant chest.

Fargo grinned as he stood and shouted back to her. "Jessie Sawyer. What the hell are you doing so far from Minnesota?"

"Missin' you, Skye honey." She was still waving, and overdid it, almost losing her balance and tottering forward out the window.

"You stay right there before you make a mess on the street, Jessie. I'll be right up," Fargo called.

"Promise?"

"Promise," he assured her with a smile.

Only then did she pull back from the windowsill and let the chintz curtains fall closed over the open window.

Damn, Fargo thought as he hurried across the street and to the front door of the establishment where Jessie was staying. It had been—he had to think about it for a while to come up with the answer—nearly three years since he'd seen Jessie. She'd been a wild one even then, headstrong, going her own way without a care in the world about what the rest of the world thought. But happily so. There wasn't a thing about her that was mean or petty. She just plain enjoyed the hell out of living. And enjoyed the things that could be done in a lifetime.

When Fargo met her, she had been a shopgirl in Little Falls. Apparently she had changed her occupation since then.

The door to the big house was opened by a maid who was dressed quite normally in a black dress and white apron—normal except that the skirt of the tight-fitting black dress came barely low enough to cover the swell of the girl's butt. It did nothing, fortunately, to conceal a pair of exceptionally pretty legs.

Fargo returned the smile she gave him, and swept his hat off.

There was nothing obvious about the front of the house, no red lantern hung, but once inside, there was no doubt that this was one high-toned and mighty fancy house of many pleasures.

The vestibule and parlor were decorated in those over-blown, overstated, plush imitations of luxury that speak of sleek women and high fees. Flocked wallpaper, velvets, brocades, gilt frames enclosing pastel portraits of attractive nudes. Fargo wouldn't claim that the place was tastefully done, but it was damned impressive.

"Good morning, sir," the maid said cheerfully. "Were you referred to us?"

"In a manner of speaking." He pointed toward the top of the winding staircase. Jessie burst into view there and raced downstairs with a squeal of delight to throw herself into Skye Fargo's arms.

The maid smiled and winked at Fargo and quietly withdrew.

"It's so *good* to see you, Skye. Honestly. Why, I didn't even know how much I've missed you until I saw you sittin' down there. Just sittin' on that bench right here in Central City, and it all come back to me then, honey, and I was so happy to see you that I could've just bawled, honey. Just bawled." She was grinning and babbling and hugging him . . . and at the same time leading him toward the stairs.

Fargo didn't mind. Not hardly. Aside from the fact that it was a pleasure to see any friendly face in this town, Jessie was always a good time.

She'd be somewhere in her twenties now, twenty-three or -four, he guessed, very much in her prime. Except for that chest of hers, she was a little bit of a thing, downright tiny. Tiny waist, round little rump, slender legs that brought the top of her head only halfway up Fargo's chest, pert features with a tip-tilted nose. But setting off the whole effect was a set of breasts like melons in August.

Judging from what he could see—and that was a fair

amount—he realized she hadn't lost any of the firmness that lent an added distinction to those breasts. Big as they were, they managed to stand proud.

Fargo bent down and kissed her. On an impulse he swept her up in his arms and carried her two steps at a time to the landing at the top of the stairs.

Jessie laughed and nuzzled her face into Fargo's neck, nibbling at him there and teasing him with her tongue.

"You'd best quit that or we aren't going to make it all the way down to your room. And then what would everyone say?"

She pulled back a few inches and tipped her face up so she could look into his eyes. "They'd say they wished they was me. That's what they'd say." She giggled and raised herself far enough to kiss him.

"You haven't changed a lick."

"O' course not," Jessie agreed. "Haven't, an' won't. You haven't neither, I'd bet."

"Not in the ways that count," he said.

"Good." She kissed him again and pointed out her room. Fargo carried her inside and used the heel of his boot to shove the door closed behind them. He took her to the big bed which was the room's dominant furnishing, and dumped her unceremoniously onto it. She let out a yelp of false anger as she bounced. As soon as she regained her balance, she stripped the chemise over her head and smiled her appreciation as Fargo stepped back to admire what she was offering him.

What she was offering him was very nice indeed. Her skin was silky and smooth and nearly without blemish. There was a tiny, crescent-shaped scar low on her belly that he didn't remember. Otherwise she seemed unchanged. Her pubic hair was a dark, thick patch of inviting fur. Her nipples were rather small and a pale, delicate shade of pink. At the moment they were erect and firm, standing out sharp and pointy on their beautifully shaped mounds.

"Oh, my," Fargo said. There was a hard, insistent bulge pushing against the buttons of his fly.

Jessie noticed his readiness and giggled again. She bounced forward to the edge of the big bed and slid off it to her knees. With a teasing grin she opened her mouth and pressed it against the cloth of his trousers, exhaling hot breath that filtered through the material to engulf and tantalize him. Fargo's reaction was a loud groan, which seemed to please her immensely.

"Something you want, honey?" she asked.

He grinned down at her. "Since the day I met you, dammit, I haven't been able to keep my hands off you. And you know it."

"So I do, Skye. That's one o' the things I just love about you. An' this here is another." Laughing, she patted his crotch, then jumped to her feet and began helping him off with his clothes.

Fargo kissed her again, and Jessie pulled him down onto the bed. They lay arm in arm for a time, tongues probing, breath mingling in their joined mouths, hands and fingers busy with mutual explorations.

Once Jessie pulled away from him and for a moment became serious. "I'm so glad to see you, Skye. I truly am." Before Fargo could ask if anything was troubling her, that impish sparkle of laughter returned to her eyes and she shoved him over onto his back. "Now you lie still there, Skye. You remember what you used t' like?"

"I couldn't forget that."

"Neither could I, honey. So you lie still an' let me." Smiling, she bent to give him a brief kiss on the lips. Then, still leaning low over him, she swayed over his torso.

Jessie kept her hair cut to a length that was perfect for the particular activity Fargo remembered so very well.

Her hair was long and loose. The curling tips of it brushed very lightly across his throat and upper chest. At the same time Jessie's nipples swept teasingly back and forth across his suddenly sensitized flesh.

Using hair and nipples at the same time she touched and tickled and pulled gently away. Back and forth. Slowly. Teasing. Tantalizing. Bringing him to rare heights of anticipation.

She bathed him with her touch from throat to chest, lingering over his nipples, covering every inch of his belly, finally lower, so slowly that he wasn't sure he could stand to wait any longer.

Once he reached for her, tried to draw her down tight against him, but Jessie laughed and pulled away, shifting her small body so that he could feel, and see, all the better.

Only when Fargo was sure he was going to embarrass himself by spurting into the air did Jessie lower herself over him so that he was into the deep, warm valley between those magnificent breasts.

She knelt above him and used her hands to press her breasts tightly together, trapping him there. It was a sweet entrapment, one Fargo didn't at all mind.

She trailed her hair lightly over his aching balls and rubbed his shaft with the enveloping flesh of her breasts.

He thought he couldn't endure much more of this teasing, but at the same time he didn't want it to end.

Without warning Jessie gave him a quick grin, ducked her head to plant a quick kiss on the engorged head of his cock, and then threw herself to the side, ending on her back with her arms and legs spread wide in welcome.

"You," Fargo said, "are marvelous." He moved onto

her . . . into her. She was as ready as he was and there was no mistaking the genuineness of her welcome.

Jessie wrapped herself tight around him and met his every motion with one of her own. . . .

Jessie sighed with contentment and snuggled herself even closer against Fargo's lean and now somewhat sweaty body. "Can't I get you something, honey? A drink? Anything at all?"

"You've already given me everything any man could want." Fargo grinned at her and playfully tweaked her right nipple. Jessie winced. "Sorry. I surely didn't mean to hurt you."

"You didn't. Not much anyhow. You know how sensitive they are anyway, an' I'm fixing to have my monthly. They get awful touchy then sometimes."

"I'll try to remember." He bent down to give her a kiss on the offended spot.

Jessie sighed again and threw an arm over his chest.

"Are you happy here?" he asked, thinking back to that one moment when he thought there might have been something wrong.

"Oh, yes. Really." She smiled. She sounded like she meant it too. "This is the nicest place in Central City. Nicest in the territory, really. The pay is wonderful. Time I'm ready to settle down, I'll have me a fine nest egg put aside. I save 'most all my money. Most o' the girls spend theirs on clothes an' stuff." She giggled. "I don't need much in the way o' clothes."

Fargo chuckled and stroked her shoulders and back appreciatively. It was true, though, that Jessie was one of those rare women who look even better without clothing than with something to cover their sags and bulges.

"An' you might not think it, but from a nice place like this one there's a lot of girls that get married. To rich men too. That's about all we get here, you know, is rich fellas.

Some o' them real nice too." She giggled. "You wouldn't believe some o' the fellas I been with here. Famous guys. Politicians. Real bigwigs, some of 'em. An' most of them tip real good. Miss Jane lets us keep all our tips, you see. The house takes part o' the regular, but we get to keep all our tips. That's how I can put so much aside—that, an' not spending it all right away."

She shook her head. "Some o' the girls, you wouldn't believe it. They think they'll go right on makin' the big money their whole lives. Me, I'm havin' fun doin' what I'm doin', and I'm not so dumb that I don't know I only got a few more years left in a place as fancy as this one. An' let me tell you, Skye, I ain't gonna let myself get put down in some cheap joint. That's how most girls end up. Won't happen to me, though. I'm not that dumb."

"You know, Jessie, there aren't very many girls I'd believe about that. But you, you're special. You're going to do just fine." He laughed. "Sure can't imagine you married and settled down, though."

"You can believe that too," she said, quite serious now. "Time comes, I'll find me the right fella, some man who's nice to be with, somebody clean an' respectable. An' let me tell you somethin' else: time I decide to settle, it'll be for good. I'll make him the best damn wife any man ever had. Nothin' on the side. Nothin' but the straight stuff. I figure to work at it, make that fella as happy as I can."

"You, my dear"—he gave her a peck on the tip of her nose—"can make a man very happy indeed."

Jessie grinned and wiggled against him. "No foolin', though, Skye. Once I decide, it'll be for keeps."

"Whoever he is, I envy him already. He's going to be one very lucky man."

She seemed pleased. She laughed. "But I ain't settled

yet, honey." She reached for him and gave an affectionate squeeze.

"Good grief, Jessie. Give me some time to rest up, will you?"

"Umm. I guess we have been pretty busy at that. It's just been so long, an' I like you so much. Forgive me?"

"Maybe. If you let me come back for more later."

"Any time, honey. You better know that."

"All right, then, it's a date."

"Listen, honey, are you hungry? I haven't had breakfast yet, except the kind you gave me, an' believe me I enjoyed that just fine, but I could sure use some groceries. Why don't you come downstairs with me an' we'll get us something to eat?"

"They won't mind?"

"Naw, it's okay. We do it sometimes for real special fellas. Might not mean all that much to the guy, of course, but the other girls know it means a fella is special when he's invited t' the kitchen." She hugged him. "Besides bein' hungry, see, it'll give me a chance to show you off. The other girls'll be so jealous! Wait an' see."

"You talked me into it."

In truth he was kind of hungry again. He and Jessie had been here for quite a while, and for most of that time the activity had been mighty vigorous. The early breakfast he'd had seemed a long time past.

Fargo dressed, with some playful hindrance from Jessie after she pulled on her chemise again and a ragged kimono, and she took him downstairs.

It was some time after noon, and now a few girls were sitting in the parlor, each of them fully dressed in elaborate gowns. The other girls were uniformly young, uniformly shapely, and all of them quite pretty. Apparently this house—Miss Jane's place, Fargo believed Jessie had said—held only the best.

The only one of them wearing anything that was at all revealing was the maid with her short skirt and stockinged legs. All of the working girls looked like they were dressed for a grand ball. Any one of them would have seemed quite comfortably in place at a St. Louis soiree.

At the moment there were three girls in the parlor, two of them reading and the third working on a piece of embroidery in a small frame, and the maid busy at something out in the foyer. Jessie led Fargo through an ornate and now empty dining room and on into the kitchen at the back of the house. The kitchen was large and had a long, rather plain table in the center.

An older woman stood by the stove. Fargo assumed that would be Miss Jane. Four more working girls were seated at the big table. Although every bit as young and attractive as the girls waiting for customers out in the parlor, these were dressed in wrappers and mules. They were without makeup, their hair not yet fixed for the day.

"We take turns with the workin' hours," Jessie explained. "All of us on durin' the evenings when things is the busiest." She took Fargo possessively by the elbow and introduced him to the other girls, adding, "You may've heard o' Skye. They call him the Trailsman."

Fargo looked at her with surprise. "I didn't think you knew that, Jessie."

She squeezed his arm. "I didn't before, but I've sure took notice whenever I've heard your name mentioned, Skye honey. I told you I've missed you. You prob'ly thought I was kidding, but I wasn't. You always been my extry-special fella."

Fargo felt inordinately pleased by that.

The girls at the table were GiGi and Yvonne and Annie and—incredibly—Miss Jane. The madame of the house was young enough and pretty enough to be one of the working girls herself. She was a tall, statuesque blonde who could not yet have seen thirty.

Of the girls only one could compare with Jessie, but she was a real stunner. Fargo wasn't sure which of them was which after the quick list of names Jessie had spouted, but this particular girl was in a class all by herself.

She was taller than most, probably five foot ten in carpet slippers, with a long, lean figure. Her hair was as black as a raven's wing and just as shiny, but her skin, flawlessly textured, was as pale and smooth as the finest porcelain. Her eyes were a bright, translucent green. Her wrapper gapped open enough that he could see a scattering of freckles low on her chest between the swell of small, taut breasts.

She was . . . It took Fargo a moment to realize that he was staring at her, trying to take in everything about this woman.

There was something—he couldn't quite define it to himself—something about her that was elegant, patrician. Something in the carriage of her head atop a long, slender neck. Something about the hollow of her cheeks, the delicate slenderness of her wrists, the full, oh-so-soft-looking shape of her mouth, the depth of those eyes.

Damn!

In spite of his recent exertions with Jessie, in spite of the fact that the delightful, pleasing Jessie was still at his side holding on to his elbow, Skye Fargo found himself wanting this woman.

He might have dug deep into his pocket, spent anything he had, paid a price beyond money to take this woman into his arms right there on the spot.

Except that Jessie was there with him, looking up now to give him a questioning, trusting look.

Fargo felt himself shudder as he tore his eyes away from the jet-haired beauty and forced a smile for Jessie.

And even then he felt a thrill of excitement at the memory of the woman.

"Now you girls keep your hands off o' Skye, hear," Jessie was saying with a peal of light, easy laughter. "Skye's my very special fella." She giggled, squeezed his elbow, and led him over to a seat at the table.

It was all Fargo could do to pay attention to Jessie and keep from staring again at the tall, slender woman at the other end of the table.

8

Fargo was downtown, back in the respectable business district of Central City, before a police tail—or someone, anyway—picked him up again. At least whoever it was, was doing a much better job of it this time. It took the Trailsman damn near a minute to spot the guy.

Nothing as obvious as a uniform this time and no one stupid enough to wallow along in plain sight. This man was medium. That was the best way to describe the very ordinary man in the very ordinary clothing: medium height, medium shade of mouse-brown hair, medium build. He could have walked into any gathering of three or more people and not be noticed. Almost anyone else in any given group of men would stand out in the memory before this fellow. In a way it pleased Fargo that whoever wanted him watched had developed enough respect for him that the job was being done right.

Actually Fargo didn't care much if he was followed or not. He was doing nothing in this town or in this territory that he was shy about having known to anyone who cared to ask. His mission for Fitzroy was a happy thing with the best of motives, and the hell with anyone who thought otherwise. The Trailsman went on about his business and pretended not to have seen the man.

At the moment Fargo's business was nothing more exciting than a bit of shopping and some supper. Jessie had put some energy into him at the lunch table and then spent the entire afternoon busily using that energy right back up again. He was just plain whipped. But nicely so, with that delightful sense of hollow satisfaction deep in his groin.

He found a general mercantile and stopped into it.

"Yes, sir," the proprietor greeted him.

"You have powder, I assume."

"Indeed we do. Anything from giant to four-F."

"Three-F is what I want, half a pound and about two pounds of lead."

The shopkeeper eyed the revolver at Fargo's belt and said, "You might be interested in cartridges. Just got a new shipment in, sent in waxed containers. I guarantee them fresh. Boxes of twenty, fifty, or a hundred."

"Guaranteed?"

"Absolutely."

"I'll take a box of fifty, then. And do you have the paper cartridges for a Sharps too?"

The man nodded. "Came in the same shipment, just as fresh."

"Two boxes of twenty of those, please."

The shopkeeper got the waxed-pasteboard containers and put them on the counter.

While Fargo was paying for his purchases, he asked the man about Margaret Fitzroy.

The man thought about it for a moment, then shook his head. "No, I don't recall seeing any new redheads in town, nor any old ones worth speaking of either. You find a few girls up on the line that henna their hair, but you can always spot that lie once they get their drawers off." He snickered and gave Fargo a wink.

"That kind isn't exactly what I'm looking for," Fargo said. "This girl's father is looking for her."

"Sorry, mister, but my answer has to be the same. I haven't seen any young lady like that. You're sure she's in town here?"

Fargo nodded. "Pulled in on the stage last night." He chose to ignore the stage agent's denials on the subject. "She was down in Georgetown and left there yesterday."

"That's a shame. She won't be so easy to find here as she woulda been down there. There's fifteen, maybe upwards of twenty thousand people in Central City. Won't be so easy to comb one particular girl out of all of them. Of course her red hair will help. Man tends to notice a redhead."

"That's what I'm counting on," Fargo said. He didn't bother to mention that he had thought the job was as good as ended once he got to Georgetown. Finding Margaret hadn't been so simple there, and the storekeeper was probably right; it would be even more difficult here. "I thank you, though."

"Any time, mister. What I don't have I can order."

"Thanks." Fargo picked up his change and left the store.

The medium-sized fellow with the forgettable features was waiting for him down the block, pretending to examine a pair of shoes in a store window. While Fargo was inside the mercantile, the man had changed from a hat to a soft cap and discarded his suitcoat in favor of a light sweater, but he would have to do better than that to become invisible. Fargo deliberately baited the tail by turning toward him and jostling him with an elbow as if by accident when he passed.

At a restaurant in the next block Fargo treated himself to a thick steak and took his time about eating it. Mr. Medium had to wait and watch from a distance while Fargo enjoyed his leisurely meal. Fargo hoped the fellow hadn't had the foresight to eat before he took up the tailing.

By the time the Trailsman was finished with his supper, it was becoming dark, and most of the stores in town had closed. It would be too late to inquire at most of the places where Margaret might have stopped for the day, so he contented himself with a tour of the hotels where a respectable single woman might stay. There were many more here than there had been in Georgetown, but he met with the same disappointingly predictable results he had gotten in the past. No one admitted to having ever seen a young woman answering Margaret Fitzroy's description.

"Damn," Fargo mumbled as he turned back across town toward his own modest hotel.

He stopped in at a saloon for a drink and didn't even bother asking there about Margaret. He was frustrated again. He stood a few spins at the Wheel of Fortune, decided this wasn't the night he was destined to get rich, and headed back out into the street.

He was more than half expecting another ambusher to greet him, but he made the rest of the trip between saloon and hotel without seeing anything more threatening than a drunk who tried to wheedle a dime out of him.

There wasn't even any sign of his tail. Probably off duty now.

Fargo yawned. A day with Jessie could take a lot out of a man. But he smiled again just thinking about her. Before she had let him go, she had made him promise to come back when he got the chance. It was a promise Fargo hadn't minded making.

The desk clerk at the hotel gave him his key, and he climbed the stairs to the second floor, a little on edge now. It wasn't impossible that whoever the overinterested party was might have found out where he was staying and be waiting for him.

But there was no one on the landing, no one in the hall. All the doors along the corridor were closed, and most of the transoms were dark, the occupants of the rooms either still out for the evening or already in bed. Fargo yawned again and fitted his key into the lock.

As the latch clicked open, the door was yanked open before him, jerking his hand forward with it, taking away from him that split second when he might have been able to draw the big Colt.

Two men swept forward out of the darkened room, grabbing for his arms and bearing him down to the hard-wood floor under their combined weight.

Fargo's arms were pinned, his hands kept carefully away from the gun. He began to kick and bite. The two had him pinned too closely for him to be able to use his hands, but to keep him from reaching his gun, they had to be pressed directly on top of him, so close together that their movements were impeded also.

Fargo tried to roll out from under them. When that failed, he faked a knee toward one man's crotch, getting him to flinch aside enough to give Fargo room to kick down and out. scraping the heel of his boot down the man's shin. The yelp of response said the kick had had the desired effect.

The second man grabbed a handful of Fargo's hair and slammed the back of the Trailsman's head against the unyielding floor.

Fargo twisted to the side and took a bite on an unwary thumb. He held on, grinding his teeth together, and the man screamed.

There was a slight loosening of the grip on Fargo's left hand. The man on that side had let go of Fargo with one hand and was trying to pluck a knife out of a sheath at his belt.

Fargo jerked his left arm free and chopped at the man's hand as the steel blade slid free of the scabbard. The edge of Fargo's hand caught the man on the wrist and the knife skittered across the floor.

Somewhere nearby a door slammed, and a man shouted for quiet. Fargo didn't have time to worry about that right now.

The second man managed to pull his hand free and tried again to grab at Fargo's hair. Fargo rose up in a head butt that took the fellow square in the face. The man began to bleed, his blood flowing hot and sticky into Fargo's eyes.

"Dammit, I said for you to quit this bullshit," a voice complained from somewhere overhead.

Fargo heard a dull thump and saw a flash of boot sole as the irate hotel guest emphasized his displeasure with a kick to one of the attacker's ribs. The man grunted and scrambled out of the way of a second kick, leaving Fargo only one attacker to cope with.

With his hands free for the first time since the two had jumped him, Fargo delivered a hard punch to the fellow's throat and gained time enough to roll aside and come to his knees. The hotel guest was still slinging his boots at the one attacker, and the second apparently wanted no part of the Trailsman when he didn't have his partner to help him. The two turned and bolted down the hall toward a back staircase, leaving Fargo and the angry hotel guest behind.

Fargo grabbed up the knife that was lying on the floor and threw it after them, but it wasn't balanced for throwing. The knife turned over lazily in the air and thudded harmlessly haft first into the shoulder of one of the men just before they disappeared in one hell of a hurry down the stairs.

Fargo bent over, gulping for breath. The tussle had been short but plenty vigorous, and he still wasn't used to the thin air at this high elevation.

"I owe you . . . some thanks . . . neighbor," he panted.

The guest responded with a hostile glare and a grunt. "I'm as pissed at you as I was at them. Man can't get any sleep around here with that kinda racket."

"I hate to say it . . . but I'm almighty glad . . . you were disturbed. I think those boys meant business."

"None of my nevermind," the unfriendly helper said. "Just keep it down from here on."

"I'm willing," Fargo told him. He'd never said a truer thing in his life. He was more than willing to be left alone, and would be more than willing to get the hell out of Central City, just as soon as he located Margaret. That couldn't happen any too soon to suit him.

"Thanks again," Fargo said.

The man grunted something unintelligible and went back inside his own room with a slam of his door.

Fargo pressed a palm to the stitch that had developed in his side and limped into his own room. He hadn't noticed any kicks or knees or whatever to his thigh during the fight but it hurt like hell now that he had a chance to pay attention. And one of them must have been punching him in the belly pretty well too.

None of it was any worse than a minor annoyance, though. He had come off lucky, thanks to that complainer from across the way.

He bolted his door behind him, checked to make sure the window was locked too, and then looked under the bed to make sure the first two hadn't left any friends behind.

Only when he was satisfied that the hotel room was as secure as he could make it did he pour water into the bedside basin and wash the blood off his face. That other fellow's blood, fortunately.

As an additional precaution he wedged the lone chair in the room under the doorknob before he stripped and got into bed and took his Colt to bed with him.

If anyone wanted to make another try for him during the night, they were going to have to come in shooting. No one was going to get close enough again to get their hands on him. And he was a light sleeper under the best of circumstances. Tonight he figured to sleep as light as goose down.

The police station was in the basement of City Hall, a narrow, three-story brick building that seemed to be making a declaration of sorts: Central City was no flash-in-the-pan mining camp; this one was already the territorial capital and intended to remain the queen city of the Colorado mining country.

It might even work out that way. The men Fargo saw going in and out of City Hall were for the most part well-dressed gentlemen in conservative suits bearing expensive stickpins and gaudy watch fobs. They seemed a cut above the usual citizens in the mining camps of Fargo's experience.

Although how they had come up with a chief of police like Big Dan Finnerty was beyond Fargo. Plain and simple politics more than likely, he decided. But then he had to admit to himself that he was hardly an impartial observer.

With a grimace Fargo crossed the hard-packed ruts of the busy street and made his way down the stone stairs into the basement of the building. A bored-looking sergeant sat behind a counter in the front room of the police station. Behind the counter two copper-buttons in none-too-clean blue coats were sharing an early-morning bucket of beer. A stench of last night's vomit came from the back of the station, probably where the night's gather of drunks was put into cells.

"Yeah?" the desk sergeant asked without interest.

"I want to see Big Dan," Fargo told him.

"The chief's busy now. What d'you want?"

"I already told you. I want to see Finnerty."

Annoyance replaced the boredom on the sergeant's features, but the man didn't care enough to make an issue of it. He used a broken fingernail to scratch some dandruff out of his mustache and then used the same finger to gesture toward a pair of armless wooden chairs in a front corner. "Wait over there."

"All right," Fargo said with a grim smile. This was their game. They certainly weren't going to make him go away that easily, no matter how long the wait. He took the indicated chair, picked up a long out-of-date newspaper from the floor, and made himself as comfortable as the hard seat and straight back permitted.

It took no particular powers of deduction to figure out which of the several doors behind the counter led to Finnerty's office. The chief's name and title were emblazoned on the wood panels in gold lettering. During the next several hours a succession of men went in and out of that office, although Finnerty himself never once put in an appearance.

Twice a uniformed officer loafing in the duty room was summoned and sent out on errands for the chief. Each time, Fargo noticed, the errand turned out to be fetching a fresh pail of beer for the chief and his current visitor.

Except for those brief contacts with the errand-runners, though, Big Dan Finnerty seemed to have no traffic with his own officers. His visitors were for the most part big-bellied, gray-haired businessmen. Or politicians. Watching the comings and goings turned out to be no irritation at all for the patient Trailsman. He was much more amused by it all than annoyed. Chief Finnerty wasn't much of a peace officer, but he was probably an accomplished ward-heeler.

Eventually the last of the morning's guests left the office, and Big Dan finally emerged in person. He had his coat on and was pulling a derby onto his head. "I'm going to lunch, Johnny. You know where to find me if you need."

The desk sergeant nodded, his eyes studiously avoiding Fargo, who was still sitting on the chair in the corner.

Fargo rose and met Big Dan at the swinging gate that separated the lobby section from the duty area in the front room.

"I've been waiting to see you," Fargo said mildly.

Finnerty gave him a cold look. "Have you, now?" He pulled a large watch from his vest pocket and snapped the cover open, making quite a show of that but barely glancing toward the time the watch indicated. "I'm busy now. Why don't you make an appointment? See Sergeant Morris there. I'm sure he will have something open."

"Yes, I'm sure he will," Fargo said agreeably. "Later this week. Early next week. Something like that."

"You'll have to excuse me now." Finnerty tried to push the gate open, found Fargo's legs blocking it, and pulled it back the other way. He was intent on getting past the Trailsman.

Fargo let him come out into the front area, then moved close and threw an arm over Finnerty's broad shoulders. From any distance at all it would have looked like a friendly and companionable gesture. What a casual observer might not have noticed, though, was the way Fargo's fingers probed into the socket above the police chief's collarbone, applying just enough pressure in that tender area to promise a great deal of pain to come. Fargo was smiling and nodding. And turning the big man toward the corner where Fargo had spent the morning waiting.

"You'd be surprised how few things I have to do, Dan. Really surprised. So why don't we have our little talk now?"

Finnerty looked toward the desk sergeant, and Fargo dug his fingers deeper into the police chief's flesh. The big man winced. He went pale with the sudden pain and his knees sagged a little. Fargo suspected it had been a very long time since Big Dan Finnerty had faced any confrontations that were directly physical, although, given his size and bulk, he had probably once been formidable in a brawl.

Fargo was still smiling at him.

Finnerty cleared his throat nervously, and the Trailsman relaxed the pressure. "Perhaps, uh, I might have a moment to spare."

"Thank you," Fargo said with exaggerated politeness. "I want to report an assault that took place at my hotel last night."

"The sergeant there can take any repor—" Fargo's fingers tightened again, and the police chief shut up.

"I want to make the report to you, Chief."

"Uh, of course. If you prefer."

"Now, Dan, I don't know what the hell is going on here. Why so many folks in town seem to have something against me. Including some of your people. But I'm getting real fed up with it. It would please me, Dan, if it all stopped. I get real tired of being shot at and jumped in the night by a bunch of thugs with knives. You know what I mean?"

"No. No, I'm afraid I don't know what you mean."

"You could even be telling me the truth, Dan, but you haven't convinced me of that. So what I'd like you to do is to call off your dogs. Or whoever's dogs. I really don't care if they belong to you or to someone else. I really don't. Just so long as they quit whatever game they're playing." Fargo didn't wait for an answer. He wouldn't have believed anything Big Dan Finnerty had to say in any event.

"I don't know and don't care what these folks think I'm doing here. I don't know and don't care what their problem is. I just don't want that to be my problem anymore. If you or anybody else wants to know what I'm doing here, all you or they got to do is ask. It isn't anything I want to hide, so I've got to assume that we have a case of mistaken identity here or mistaken intentions, whatever. I'm just trying to do a favor for a man, just trying to find a gentleman's daughter so a family can get back together again. There's nothing secret about that, nothing sinister, nothing that is a threat to anybody, not here or anyplace else. Do you understand that, Dan?''

''Uh, mister, whoever you are . . . I really don't know what you're talking about. I have no knowledge of any of this.''

''Of course you don't, Dan. Just like you haven't had me followed. Just like you don't know anything about whoever is behind these boys that're always waiting for me. We'll leave it at that. We'll just say that you've done your civic duty by being polite and listening to a stranger. If you want to pass the information along to wherever it will do some good, that's up to you. But I think you should remember something, Dan: I'm starting to get really angry about this whole thing, and you are the only guy in town that I'd know to take it out on if I get pushed too far. You know?'' Fargo was still smiling, his voice low and almost gentle. But the menace of it came through quite clearly.

''I don't think—''

Fargo didn't want to listen. He squeezed Big Dan's shoulder and patted the beefy chief in a most friendly manner. ''Go have yourself a nice lunch now, Dan. Thanks for your time.''

Fargo turned and walked out of the police station without looking back. It was time to get back to business.

He had already checked the hotels in his search for Margaret Fitzroy. Now he inquired at the boarding houses, the shops where a young woman might look for work, at the cafés where a cook might be needed. Finally at the two schools on the theory that an unattached young woman might very well be a schoolteacher. There were few enough occupations open to a single woman, and he tried to cover them all.

The results of his afternoon searching, though, were entirely too familiar. No one knew Margaret. No one had seen her. No one had heard anything about the arrival in town of a young woman answering her description. Fargo's frustration combined with his anger at the repeated assaults.

He still couldn't figure out why someone was after him. It could have nothing to do with his search for Margaret Fitzroy. He was convinced of that. Someone must have mistaken him for someone else, someone who was a threat to some one or some thing here in Central City. If that were so, simple denials probably wouldn't be enough to turn them aside, no matter what he said to Dan Finnerty or anyone else. Still, he had felt he had to at least try. He just doubted it had done any good.

He had supper at an inexpensive restaurant frequented by miners, then stopped in at the livery to check on the black-and-white Ovaro.

After so much rest and grain, the horse looked fit and full of energy. Fargo wished he could say as much for himself. This job was wearing at him, and for the first time since he had undertaken it he considered giving up. Not to find Margaret and return her to her father's love but simply to get away from Central City.

The Ovaro stamped impatiently at the straw bedding in the box stall.

"You and me both," Fargo said. He scratched the big horse's poll and rubbed the deep hollow under his jaw, then gave him a final pat and turned to leave the livery barn.

Skye headed for the front door, then on an impulse turned and went back the way he had just come, toward the wide doors leading out to the corral. It was rarely wise to leave a building, or any place, by the same route one used to enter. The Trailsman's caution had long since become habit, and now he had good reason to be wary.

He ducked through the corral rails and made his way slowly through the broad-rumped draft horses and the cat-hammed, skinny, impossibly tough mules that were contained there. He clucked softly to them as he moved. Most of the draft stock were so weary from their day's labors that they barely noticed his passage. One mule laid its ears back and tried to kick him, but its heart wasn't in the effort and Fargo sidestepped the hoof easily. "Better luck next time, old fellow," he crooned. The mule pinned its ears again but turned away.

The back of the livery corral met a narrow, garbage-strewn alley that ran behind the nearby businesses. Space level enough to build on was at a premium here. Craggy mountain peaks hung over the town in all directions, the mountainsides littered with dark, gaping tunnel entrances and pale, fan-shaped rock slides where waste rock had been dumped. Whatever foliage there might have been here before the valuable ores were found, there was nothing now, hardly a sprig of green anywhere in sight. Trees and even shrubs had been cut for fuel and shoring timbers. Fargo was beginning to think that this country could be damned well depressing.

He ducked through the corral rails again and entered the alley. It was evening, but there was a little light left in the sky. He hadn't seen the sun itself since it dropped behind the mountain peaks about midafternoon, but a little of its light remained.

Fargo picked his way through the decomposing trash in the alley until he reached the next side street and took that back toward the street where the livery was situated. He stopped just short of the corner, removed his hat, and then eased forward, pretending to be loafing against the corner of the building there.

His lips tightened into a grim line at what he saw.

No one on the street seemed to be paying any attention

to the front of the livery barn, but directly across the street from the barn a man was sitting in a rocking chair on a second-story balcony.

The man sat in the twilight with his hat pulled low over his eyes and a blanket laid over his lap.

From this distance and angle Fargo couldn't see clearly, but he thought there was a suspiciously flat object held beneath that blanket. A shotgun, perhaps, or a carbine.

Anyone incautiously leaving the front of that barn, particularly if the intended victim paid attention only to the ground level, would be a sitting duck for a gunman on that balcony.

And it would be only reasonable for someone to figure that Fargo would return now and then to check on his horse.

A cold anger drew the Trailsman's muscles tight, and the surface of his lake-blue eyes froze over.

Skye Fargo had had just about enough.

He turned and went back toward the string of alleys that lay behind the street-front buildings. A few blocks down, it should be safe enough to cross to the other side of the street and make his way back through the alleys to a point behind that building where the man in the rocking chair waited on the balcony.

It was time, Fargo figured, to get some answers.

He turned and began his slow, patient stalk.

It was difficult to know which building was which from the alley, but he had to be sure. Showing up on the wrong balcony could get a man shot. Or let the watcher get away. Fargo intended to get some answers about who wanted him . . . and why.

He counted the back doors down from the end of the block, checked yet again to make sure, and slipped inside the unlocked door, his Colt already in his hand.

The door opened into a kitchen. The building was yet

another of the many boardinghouses in the town. The boarders probably were at supper. The oven threw off a strong heat and there was a smell of roasted meat in the close atmosphere of the kitchen. Serving dishes were piled in a washtub on the counter near the oven, and some mostly empty pie tins were set on the worktable. Fortunately the kitchen was empty at the moment, but Fargo could hear conversation from the other side of a swinging door, presumably leading into the dining room.

He thought at first that he might have to walk brazenly past the boarders, then he saw a small door off to the side of the interior wall. It opened onto a dark, narrow set of service stairs. Perfect.

Moving on tiptoe, ears attuned to the faintest whisper, Fargo mounted the stairs, with Colt at the ready. The ambusher might have grown tired of waiting and be on his way down. Fargo held to the edge of the treads to avoid squeaks and creaks.

The staircase ended at a hallway that ran the length of the second floor. Bedroom doors, most of them standing open, faced both sides of the hall.

Fargo inched forward, trying to judge the remembered distance from the south wall of the building to the balcony where his man waited in the rocking chair.

This one, he thought. The door, as he would have expected, was closed. A tight smile flattened his lips as he turned the knob—it was unlocked—and eased the door open.

The man in the rocking chair was not more than a dozen feet in front of him now, his back to Fargo. French doors led from the bedroom onto the balcony.

My turn, Fargo breathed silently to himself as he inched forward.

He took his time about it. The man was there, facing out toward the front door of the barn, his rocking chair motionless and his head tipped forward as if in sleep. He obviously had heard nothing yet, and the Trailsman didn't intend for him to. Fargo didn't want to shoot him. Not yet anyway. He wanted a few minutes' conversation first. Then if the man wanted trouble, Skye would be glad to give him all he wanted.

The Trailsman reached the French doors in utter silence. The man in the rocking chair hadn't moved. He continued to look down toward the livery barn where Fargo might have been expected to appear.

One more slow, cautious step forward in silence.

Then, with an unnerving shout, Fargo crossed the last remaining distance between them and shoved the cold steel muzzle of his Colt hard into the man's right ear. "Move, you bastard, and you're dead on the spot."

The man's head jerked upright and his eyes snapped open. "My God, Jesus, save me!" His hands flew out from under the blanket across his knees and met above his heart. The man in the rocking chair was white-haired and feeble. He'd been sound asleep in the chair.

"Oh, Lordy," Fargo said in confusion. He could see now that the object that was hidden under the blanket was long and flat indeed, but it was no shotgun or carbine. It was nothing more threatening than a walking cane. "Lordy," Fargo repeated.

The old man looked scared out of his wits, and quick tears came to his rheumy eyes. "I haven't any money. I swear that I haven't," he blurted in terror. "But there's a watch on my dresser. It's only brass, but it must be worth something. Please don't hurt me. That's all I have. Please." His chin was quivering and he was crying freely now, not listening, too intent on his own fear to hear as Fargo tried to stammer out an apology.

"I can't . . . Forgive me, mister. Please forgive me. I thought . . ."

It took Fargo a good five minutes to calm the poor old fellow and get him to listen to an explanation that sounded inexcusably weak. At last the old boy did seem to be recovering from the shock Fargo had given him.

Fargo leaned on the rail of the balcony and surveyed the street below him.

No one had been waiting for him outside the livery this time, which only meant that they hadn't thought of it yet, or hadn't identified the Trailsman's distinctively marked Ovaro . . . yet. Whoever *they* were.

Jesus, Fargo told himself, shaken. He might have killed the old man by provoking heart failure if not with the swift Army Colt.

The old gentleman compounded Fargo's sense of guilt by offering the Trailsman forgiveness if not understanding.

Yes, it was all right, perfectly all right. He had just gotten such a start, hadn't been prepared . . . But it was all right now.

As soon as the fright was over, the explanations offered, and both men's heartbeats had returned to something like normal, the old gentleman began to pratter, obviously pleased to have a captive listener no matter how he had acquired that pleasure.

And Skye Fargo hadn't the heart to disappoint the old fellow by leaving him alone again now.

The old man talked into the night, his eyes too weak and the growing darkness too dense for him to see Fargo any longer, but content as long as he knew there was someone close by to listen.

He was sixty-eight years old, and could Fargo believe that? Of course not. He was in fine shape for a man his age, wasn't he? But they'd retired him. He'd come west to be close to his son. The son was married now. Hadn't much time for his father. The old fellow droned on into the night.

Fargo listened with half an ear at first, then with genuine attention and sympathy.

If his own father had lived, if there had never been any reason for the Trailsman to be born into his private world of hate and grief and vengeance, would Fargo ever have permitted his own father to become as alone as this poor fellow was?

It was a question that could never have any real answer, something Fargo would never honestly know. That opportunity had been forever denied to the man called the Trailsman.

Finally the old gentleman's voice wound down, needing his rest now more than his chance to talk about himself.

"Are you sure you're all right now?" Fargo asked.

"I'm fine. All over it."

"If there's anything I can do, any way I can make up to you for this . . ."

"No, I'm fine now. But anytime you want to talk, son, you come see me. Anytime at all. Always here, you know. Be a pleasure to see you again." The old fellow cackled hollowly. "But mind you come a little louder next time. Knock on the door or something."

"If I can, I'll do that, sir."

"Anytime." The old man's voice trailed off into a whisper and his chin sagged down toward his chest.

Fargo tiptoed away from the balcony as silently as he had approached it, although for a greatly different reason.

If he did have a chance to come back, he decided, he was going to have to find out who the old man's son was. Go and have a talk with that one. It mightn't do any good. But it might make Skye Fargo feel better about things.

9

Fargo made his way through the back streets of town, heading toward the whorehouse where Jessie worked.

It wasn't so much a desire for sex that drove him toward her. At least not for that alone. He felt a strong desire now to hold a woman. And to be held. He felt a need for human touch, and there was no other way he knew to get it. So he moved across town in a hurry.

But not in so much of a hurry that he became incautious. Just because one man hadn't meant him harm it didn't necessarily follow that no one did. He still had to worry about whoever was after him. The Trailsman could seldom relax his constant wariness.

He avoided the busy main streets where anyone watching for him might be and reached the house without incident. The place was brightly lighted behind tightly drawn draperies. Checking once again to make sure he wasn't followed, he approached the door and knocked.

For nearly a full minute he heard nothing, then the staccato *tock-a-tock* of a woman's footsteps. The door was opened, not by the maid Fargo expected to see but by the tall, dark-haired beauty who had captivated his attention when Jessie took him down to lunch yesterday.

She had been extraordinarily beautiful then in a casual wrapper and without makeup. Tonight she was beyond beauty. She was exquisite. She belonged not in some Central City whorehouse but in a masterwork of art. On canvas. Sculpted in the finest marble. Standing in front of her, Fargo felt suddenly shy and awkward, like a boy fallen in love with his schoolteacher.

Her hair was piled and pinned in a high upsweep, emphasizing the slender column of her neck and the vulnerability of her throat.

Her gown was full in the skirt and swept the floor but cut low in the bodice, allowing him to see the pale perfection of her skin while exposing only a hint of breast-swell— revealing nothing, suggesting everything. Her eyes, under curiously dark and highly arched brows, were a brighter, clearer green than he remembered.

"Yes?" The single word was delivered in a voice low and faintly husky, cool but at the same time inexpressibly seductive. For a moment Skye Fargo, the Trailsman, the master of wilderness and horses and women across a wide, wide land, was taken completely aback, at a loss for words.

"Ah, yes," the woman said. "You would be dear Jessie's laddie. Come in." She held the door wider, and Fargo went inside.

"I uh . . ." He had come here to see Jessie, dammit, but it was this woman's beauty that was causing the swelling at his groin.

"Of course," the woman said, as if he were making sense. "But didna Jessie tell you? She's started her delicate time of the month and will be unable to receive gentlemen visitors for a few days."

The maid came down the stairs to take Fargo's hat and carry it out of sight. While she was doing that, the tall whore stood back and gave Fargo a looking-over. She did it with bold thoroughness, running those lovely eyes up his legs, across the bulge at his crotch and the narrowness of his hips, over the lean belly and the breadth of his chest and shoulders, finally reaching the hank of raven hair that spilled down over his lake-blue eyes. There was something in the depths of her green eyes that hinted of approval.

"Might I accommodate you?" The invitation was delivered in a low and gentle voice but with a hint of mockery underlying the surface. She knew there could be no rejection of any offer.

This woman simply didn't know rejection. It would serve her right if he turned and walked right out of here. But even while he was thinking that, he was busy thinking up excuses for Jessie. She was ailing. She had said herself just yesterday that she was coming to that time of the month, so she couldn't be with him anyway. Surely she wouldn't object now if he was with another woman—with *this* woman. Hell, he made no objection to her going with every man who met her price. How could she mind him going with this woman now that Jessie couldn't?

Well before Fargo had his rationalization worked out, the beautiful whore had already taken him by the hand and was leading him toward the staircase.

Fargo's basic honesty came to the fore and he admitted to himself that he need not have bothered trying to work out any reasoning to justify sleeping with this woman. She had such a powerful effect on him that he wasn't sure he would have been able to resist if Jessie had been standing right there beside them begging him not to go.

"My fee is fifty dollars, laddie," she said bluntly as she led him up the curving stairs. Her manner was quite matter-of-fact, even though such a fee for a whore's services was staggering.

A cowhand's normal pay was twenty dollars for a full month's work. A miner working the stopes nearby might make twice that. For either one of them fifty dollars would be the wages of weeks of hard effort.

The sensible, rational, logical thing to do would be to laugh in the woman's face, turn, and leave.

Instead, Fargo was feeling pleased that Fitzroy had been so generous with the advance he had paid. The Trailsman had the money to meet the fee. He never even considered refusing to pay it.

She led him to the top of the stairs. Fargo looked rather nervously in the direction of Jessie's room, willing her to remain behind the closed door, and was grateful when the woman led him in the opposite direction.

Her room was as elegant as her beauty. It was furnished not in the florid styles of Cat-house Plush but with simple understatement. It suited her.

She smiled at him as she reached around him, the fingers of one hand lightly brushing over his chest, and slid the bolt closed on the door and locked them into delicious privacy. Her perfume was as delicate as the flawless texture of her skin.

Fargo wanted to grab her, crush her in his arms, and love her right there on the floor. He restrained himself only because he was beginning to feel like something of an idiot. He'd hardly said two coherent words—come to think of it, maybe hadn't said *that* much since she opened the door downstairs.

"Would you like a drink first?" She smiled, the expression changing the shape of her lips but failing to reach her eyes. "I don't care to rush, do you, laddie?"

"I can think of better ways to make it last."

This time her expression—of amusement—did reach her eyes. She laughed softly and said, "Aye, laddie, so can I." She reached up to give him a brief, open-mouthed kiss with lips as soft as a wisp of morning mist on still water.

He reached for her, but she had already turned and was

gliding away across the room. Tantalized, Fargo began to shed his clothing.

The elegant whore was just as quick getting out of her gown and stockings. She made no particular attempt to be provocative about it, but she was so beautiful and so graceful that any motion she made would almost have to be an exercise in seduction. Fargo's erection rose, insistent.

Clothed she was beautiful; nude she was perfection. Her limbs were long and slim, wrists and ankles so tiny they appeared fragile. Fargo thought he could span her waist within his hands, and her belly was flat. Her breasts weren't large, but high and unusually firm, with small, pale nipples tilted upward. They seemed in absolutely perfect proportion to her size and her shape. She undressed with her back to him, then turned to face him with her hands clasped together and held low in front of her pubic bush. It was an odd pose for her to adopt, he thought. Certainly no woman in her position could be afflicted by any sense of modesty. Not that he gave a damn.

He crossed the room to her and took her roughly by the shoulders. She looked at him in wide-eyed silence as he crushed his mouth against hers. She was unresponsive, as cold as she was beautiful. Her lips and her body were pliant—he could do with her as he wished—but she was unresponsive.

That, finally, broke the spell she had cast on him.

Fargo pulled away from her and peered deep into those huge, undeniably beautiful eyes. Beautiful they were, but whatever was behind them was held in close privacy, not to be shared. Whatever was there wasn't his to claim.

"Thanks, but no thanks," he said. He turned toward the chair where he had put his clothes and began dressing.

"Wait!" There was emotion in her voice now, and oddly it wasn't curiosity that he was choosing to leave but a genuine note of distress that he would have decided to do so. "Wait."

"No," Fargo said sadly. "I came here to see Jessie. That part was a good idea. Coming up here with you"—he shook his head—"that wasn't so damn smart. Jessie's sweet. A man doesn't just buy her body. When she's with a man, little Jessie gives of herself. She mightn't be as pretty as you are. Except for one place. And that's inside, down where it really counts. So I'll be leaving now, and I thank you for the lesson you've taught me."

"You can't go," she said.

"The fifty dollars, right?" Fargo barked out a sharp, bitter sound that might have been a laugh. "All right. A man ought to be willing to pay for his higher education." He buttoned his jeans and reached deep into his pocket. He pulled out a pair of double eagles and an eagle and tossed them onto the unused bed. Then with a cold look at the beautiful whore he dug down into his pocket again. "And something extra for your trouble," he said. He threw beside the gleaming gold coins one more, a copper two-cent piece.

With a cry that sounded like anguish the tall, lovely woman dashed toward him.

Fargo thought for a moment that she was going to slap or scratch him in a fit of pique. Instead, she ran past him. To the bed.

Surely, he thought, she couldn't be so damned greedy that she wanted to grab those coins before he could take them back.

But she ignored those too, bypassing them just as she had rushed past him, and began to dig under the dust ruffle that bordered the thick mattress.

"What . . . ?"

Then he saw what she'd been after. When she straightened and turned, she had a wicked, slim-bladed dirk in her hand. She held it inexpertly and raised it foolishly high before she struck out at him.

Son of a bitch, he thought.

There was something else here, something that was fighting for his attention, but right now he couldn't take the time to worry about it. That could wait.

The knife blade flashed down and forward, aimed with unexpected speed and strength straight for the Trailsman's heart.

Fargo's hand flashed up to intercept the blow. He grabbed her wrist and bore down, hard, twisting and applying pressure. The fact that she was a female cut no ice when the woman had a knife in her hand and was trying to bury it in his chest.

She cried out and went to her knees, dropping the dirk and grabbing at Fargo's wrist with her free hand. "You're hurting me," she complained.

"Do tell. And I suppose you weren't trying to hurt me what that little playtoy?"

She frowned but said nothing more.

Fargo reached down to retrieve the fallen knife, took a moment to admire its workmanship, and then set it down on the floor again with the front third or so of the blade laid over the side of a shoe. A hard stamp of his heel over the hilt snapped the tempered blade, making the thing useless as a weapon. He kicked the pieces of broken knife under the bed and dragged the whore to her feet.

"I think we need to have a talk," he said.

She was beautiful. Lordy, even if she had just tried to kill him, she was still just about the prettiest woman he'd ever seen. He stood over her, unable to avoid admiring that gorgeous, naked body.

That was what was bothering him. When he stood there looking her over, he could see what he had missed before, what she had been hiding from him with her hands after she undressed.

Her hair was a gleaming, glossy black, as dark as Fargo's own. On top of her head, that is.

But down below her pubic hair was a close-cropped tuft of bright, bright red.

"Son of a bitch," Fargo breathed, comprehension coming to him. "They call you Annie, don't they? Annie Roy."

The woman gave him a look that was half-frown, half-pout.

"You dyed your hair, didn't you? To keep me from recognizing you as Margaret Fitzroy."

At the sound of the name "Fitzroy" the pout in her expression changed to fear, but Fargo was so elated by his discovery that the knowledge barely registered.

"No damn wonder I couldn't find you. Not down in Georgetown and not when I got here. I was looking for you in all the places a respectable single girl might be. All the shops, all the hotels and boardinghouses and places a young lady out on her own might be expected to look for work. Damn me, I never once thought to look for you in places like this."

Margaret Anne turned her head away, refusing to look him in the eyes.

"If you hadn't been so damn pretty, you could've got away with it, too. Damn near did anyhow. No wonder people remember you for a long time after they've seen you. I sure will, even if you did try to kill me." He pulled her over to the edge of the bed and sat her down on it, sitting beside her so that he could continue to hold her captive by the wrist. She had tried once to kill him. He wasn't going to turn her loose now.

"Why'd you do that, anyway? I've meant you no harm, Margaret. I only want—"

"Bastard." She spat the word at him. "What are you waiting for? Go ahead. Get it over with." Anger and then

151

fear turned to defiance in those large green eyes. "Go ahead, you son of a bitch. Look me right in the eyes and get it over with. What will it be, killer? Are you going to strangle me? Stab me? How?"

"What in the hell are you talking about?" He was genuinely puzzled. As he listened to her, to the tone of her voice, and looked into those large, beautiful eyes, there was no doubt that she genuinely believed what she was saying. "I didn't come here to hurt you."

She snorted her disbelief of that statement. "Sure. You came here to help me, didn't you?" She sounded bitter now. "That's what you've been telling people, isn't it? That you came here to reunite me with my father?"

"You heard, then?" he said. "You knew I was looking for you?"

"Of course I knew, you bastard. Why do you think I'm working here?"

"What does that have to do with anything?"

Her only answer was another snort of bitter derision.

"Whoa. Wait a minute here. I know you don't believe me. Not any more than I figured to believe you a minute ago. But you aren't in any hurry to be killed, surely. So humor me. Make believe I don't know what in hell you're talking about, which I don't, whether you know it or not. Tell me what in the name of Hades you're talking about."

Margaret gave him a look of frank suspicion. But then she looked down at the iron grip Skye had on her wrist and realized she wasn't going anywhere until or unless he permitted her to do so. She took a deep breath.

And then she began to talk, slowly and with closely guarded caution at first, then more freely as she warmed to the subject and seemed to forget the dangers she felt herself to be in.

Margaret Anne Fitzroy-Powell was a very frightened young woman. Someone—and she certainly believed

Skye Fargo to be with him or them—was trying to kill her. The first attempt on her life had taken place in Virginia City. She survived that attack only through the intervention of an admirer who happened to be with her at the time. She survived, but her beau did not.

The second attempt was also made in Virginia City. Thoughts that the first incident had been an isolated, random act by a criminal with no particular victim in mind were dispelled without question by the second incident. She escaped by an accident of fortune into an alley and then into the haven of a back door. The door had led into the kitchen of one of the whorehouses of Virginia City.

The madame of the house had offered her a continuing form of refuge by way of employment.

Alone by then, without family or prospects, she had only her beauty to trade on. And she was no virgin. She had been intimate with several young men of the camp. She enjoyed the sexual contact, she admitted freely to the Trailsman. She considered her options, particularly those weighted by her fears of whoever was attempting to kill her, and accepted the offered job. Quickly judged to be a "fancy" in the marketplace, she commanded the highest fees in the short history of the camp.

But her disappearance from the public streets didn't protect her. Whoever it was who wanted her killed was persistent. The third attempt was made by way of a bomb placed in the kitchen of the whorehouse. Two girls died in that explosion. Margaret Anne escaped, shaken and temporarily deafened but still alive.

She fled south to Cherry Creek. She knew she would need both income and protection and sought out a powerful political figure in the territory who happened also to control several of the better houses in Cherry Creek and the mining camps in the mountains to the west. She had, in effect, sold herself in exchange for protection.

That, Fargo realized now, explained the time lapse between when Margaret left Virginia City and when that stage agent said she arrived in Georgetown.

When Fargo showed up in Georgetown asking questions about her, her protector moved her to Miss Jane's Central City house, run by Miss Jane but owned by the gentleman from Cherry Creek.

"Is it some of his people who've been after me, then?"

Margaret Anne shrugged, quite obviously not caring if anyone wanted to kill this man who had been looking for her. "I couldn't say that for sure," she said. "I know that my . . . friend . . . is aware of you. And I know that he doesn't want me moved from this house. I'm doing awfully well here already. I make a lot of money for him."

Fargo could certainly believe that. She was still the most beautiful woman he could remember seeing. With or without clothing. Having her sitting there beside him, naked and lovely, was becoming damned uncomfortable. His erection was back, stronger than ever.

"Listen, Margaret. I don't know anything about whoever it is who tried to kill you before. Whoever they were and whatever they wanted, I'm not connected with them in any way. I was hired to find you. Not to hurt you." He spoke slowly and gently, almost desperately willing her to see and to hear the sincerity in his eyes and in his voice. "That's all," he said, "Just find you. They call me the Trailsman. Jessie told you that. And that is what I am as well as who. I've killed men, true, but I am no killer. There isn't enough money to hire me to shoot someone down without just cause. I couldn't do it. That isn't the way my father raised me to be. And now I've been hired to return you to your own father, who loves and misses you. And that, I swear to you, is all I was hired to do."

She looked at him, a long, searching look direct into his blue eyes. Then she looked away in indecision. "Jessie said your name is Fargo?"

"Yes. Skye, if you prefer."

"I'd like to believe you, Skye. I really would."

"You must believe me, Margaret. It's the simple truth."

"You say it like it really is, at least as far as you know, the truth," she acknowledged. She was looking straight into his eyes again. "I think . . . I know I want to believe you. I know Jessie believes in you completely. She even loves you in her own sweet way." Margaret sighed. "I talked to her about you. And then I had her sent down to Georgetown to get her out of the way so I could get you up here and . . . and get to you before you killed me. I didn't know my employer was already trying to do that for me." She shuddered.

"I hate violence, Skye. Toward anyone. But I felt like I hadna a choice. Jessie told me I was wrong about you. I didna believe her."

Now and then, Fargo noticed, a hint of accent kept creeping into her voice. That should have tipped him to her before, perhaps, but he hadn't thought it significant.

"But . . ." Her wrist turned in his grasp. He allowed it this time; she was no longer his prisoner but a beautiful young woman who sat with the weight of fear and uncertainty on her slim shoulders, holding his hand.

"I want to trust you, Skye. But you've been lied to at the very least, even if you are trying to do only the best."

"I don't understand."

She turned her head and gave him a wide-eyed, solemnly innocent look. "You say you want to reunite me with my father, Skye."

"That's right."

"But, you see . . . my father is dead."

"Don . . ." He was thinking about Powell, her stepfather. Margaret shook her head. "Not Donnie. Although he's dead too, of course. The thing is, my mother was a widow when she married Donnie Powell. My *real* father died many years ago.''

''Your real father . . . ?'' Fargo was stunned by Margaret's statement. Her father dead? Then who the hell was the Trailsman working for?

''That's right. Daddy died when I was three years old. Mama married Donnie when I was, oh, seven, something like that. Just a minute.'' She got up and crossed the room to a large, fancy chiffonier. She pulled open the top drawer and brought out a gray pasteboard folder that she carried back to the bed and handed to Fargo.

The Trailsman, however, was quite frankly distracted by the sight of all that naked, elegant loveliness in motion. His erection was back and becoming distinctly uncomfortable despite the seriousness of their conversation.

He opened the folder and found it to be a daguerreotype that was remarkably like the one Fitzroy had shown him back in St. Louis. Except that this one was a portrait not of a small child but of a young, handsome, stiffly posed couple probably in their mid-twenties and wearing clothes that were fashionable a generation past.

''My parents,'' Margaret said. ''That is my real daddy with Mama. Before she met Donnie.''

''I'll be damned,'' Fargo whispered.

The portrait was at least twenty years old. But there was no doubt in his mind, none whatsoever, that the man in that picture was *not* the man who had introduced himself as this girl's father.

''What?'' Margaret asked.

He explained.

''Of course that man couldn't have been. I already told you, my father died. We lived in New York then. Daddy was sailing. His boat overturned and he drowned.''

''New York,'' Fargo said. ''That's where this . . . this man who claimed to be your father, that is where he said he lived. I don't suppose . . ." He shook his head. The thought occurred to him that if no body had been found, perhaps Margaret's father hadn't died after all. Perhaps he really had abandoned his family. But that held no water either, because the man who had approached Fargo in St. Louis was certainly not the man whose finely chiseled features peered out of the fading portrait the girl kept.

"I don't pretend to understand any of this," Fargo said, "but I can promise you one thing, Margaret: I mean you no harm, and if there is anything I can do about it, no one else is going to harm you either."

Margaret—he persisted in thinking of her as the orphaned Margaret Fitzroy instead of the high-priced whore Annie Roy—slipped her hand into his and leaned against his shoulder.

"Look, uh"—he cleared his throat with some degree of difficulty—"I know this isn't exactly an appropriate time. But you are awfully pretty. And awfully naked. And, well . . ."

Margaret laughed and put her arms around him. "And you, Skye, are every bit as fine a man as Jessie said you were. And it certainly isn't like I was a virgin. And I'd like to be held right now. If you wouldna mind."

"Mind? Not hardly."

He was facing her as they spoke. And it seemed the most natural thing possible that his head dipped foward just as hers rose to meet him.

Her lips were as soft as the promise of their full, lovely appearance. He kissed her gently, without heat or hunger for the moment, giving her time to respond.

She did so, and Skye discovered that there was nothing cold or distant about this regal-looking young woman.

She had said she enjoyed being with a man. Now he believed it.

Tall as she was, Margaret was a perfect match for Fargo's whipcord height and lean, hard body.

They lay back on the big bed, twined closely together, in no hurry now, exploring, touching, tasting, and feeling. Her body was like cool satin against his flesh when she helped him out of his clothes for the second time that evening and lay in his arms.

Margaret's breath was as sweet as her perfume. Sweeter, perhaps, because it was real and the perfume was artifice.

He bent lower and began to tease her nipples—so pale and so small, yet so perfect—with the tip of his tongue.

Margaret shuddered with pleasure and stroked the back of his head, tangling her fingers in his hair and running one long, tantalizing nail inside his ear. "You are quite a man, Skye Fargo," she whispered.

Fargo was too busy to answer. He fondled her breasts gently, coaxing and encouraging her, and her hand crept down between their bodies to lightly grasp and stroke him.

Fargo licked and nibbled and touched, slowly and gently, first here and then here, until she was moist and ready for him. She sighed with pleasure as he raised himself over her, and she opened herself to receive him, her arms and long, slim legs wrapping tight around him. He lowered himself onto her and into her and felt her quickened breath warm in the hollow of his neck.

She was kissing him, licking him, probing lightly into his ear with her warm, active tongue. "Now, Skye. Please."

He began to move within her, slowly at first and then with harder, faster strokes as her body demanded more and more of his.

Margaret Fitzroy or Annie Roy, this woman was everything any man could dream of.

Fargo sat up, propped on a huge mound of feather pillows against the headboard. He felt sated, hugely content. So, he guessed, did Margaret. She smiled at him and cuddled against his side.

"I've been thinking," he said.

"So have I," she answered with a smile. She reached down to cup his balls in the warmth of her hand and give him a gentle squeeze.

"Haven't you had enough of that yet?"

"No," she said with an impish grin.

"Good, because I haven't either. But that isn't what I was thinking about."

"You're going to insist on telling me, aren't you?"

"Uh huh. Business first. Then we'll play some more."

"All right. If you can keep your mind on business." She had a feline, canary-eating smile on her lovely face.

"I've been thinking that there might be a way to sort this thing out. Figure out why I was really hired to track you down, and . . ." Fargo was finding Margaret's ability to distract somewhat stronger than his own ability to concentrate. She had started at his chest, using nothing but the tip of her tongue. That had been hard enough to cope with. But now that warm, soft, active thing had fallen considerably south of his chest. And he kept losing his train of thought.

With a groan he gave in to the inevitable, closed his eyes, and let the damned girl have her way with him. It was nearly an hour later before he could get his mind back on business again. But then he went on like there had been no interruption whatsoever.

"I've been thinking," he said, "that we might be able to shake this fake Fitzroy out of the woodwork if I send him the message that he's expecting. Tell him that I've found you but that I can't convince you to come to him. Better yet, I'll tell him that I found you but haven't approached you yet, that I think he should come and decide for himself whether he wants to see you. Your working here, well, I sure hell don't have anything against it. But an easterner would likely think that was a goodenough reason for me to want to talk to him before anything is said to you. Of course, you'd have to hide. Your, uh, employer's bullyboys might be able to protect you, but I wouldn't want to count on that. But I think we can find a way to keep you safe until we get that worked out permanent.''

"Thinking of that," Margaret said, "I'm going to have to get them called off you, Skye. Honestly I had no idea that they were trying to kill you."

Fargo grunted. "This employer of yours must have a lot of pull. He even has the local police helping him."

"Big Dan? He thinks he's in love with me anyway. He gets girls free three nights a week, kind of as a favor, and he always picks me." She made a face.

No wonder, Fargo agreed. He couldn't imagine a beautiful woman like Margaret under that gross, grunting son of a bitch. But that was her business and none of his, thank goodness.

"I wouldn't object, actually, to having those particular dogs called off me and put to guarding you from this phony father of yours. We'll get that done first if you don't mind, then see if we can't smoke the boyo out of the bushes."

Margaret sighed and nuzzled his chest. "Actually," she said, "I am rather glad that I didna kill you, Mr. Fargo."

"Actually," he said, "I agree."

10

A telegraph line, shakily built and not always safe from Indian depredations but functioning most of the time, had been extended to the territorial capital, so Fargo was able to send his wire to New York City as soon as the office opened for business the next morning. He got it off, using the corporate address the alleged Fitzroy had given him, and went back to Miss Jane's to have breakfast with Margaret. He had spent the night there with her and was tired as hell this morning, but he didn't mind that in the slightest.

She gave him a kiss of greeting when he joined her in the kitchen, and that brought a round of eyebrow raising from the other girls. Apparently it was unheard of for one man to be the "special fella" of two different girls in the same house. Miss Jane, at least, didn't share their surprise. Margaret had already put her in the know when she called the ambushers off Fargo's back.

The cook served up a huge meal. Apparently these working girls developed appetites from their labors that would have done a lumberjack proud. Fargo enjoyed the sights around him as well as the eatables: the working girls weren't especially noted for modesty during their leisure hours.

But he had to concede that he was already with far and away the finest of the lot. There was no temptation here for any changing of horses midstream.

"The way I see it," Fargo said when he and Margaret were alone again, "we have a couple weeks at the earliest before Fitzroy . . ." Margaret gave him a dirty look. "All right, then, before this man who calls himself Fitzroy could get out here from New York. And that's if he's awfully lucky with his connections. There are rails laid for maybe half the trip and the connections are pretty spotty at times. Then he'd have to change to a fast coach, and that's if he is lucky enough to find one. I wouldn't expect an answer to my wire for probably three or four days, and by then he should be on his way already. Are you sure you don't want to reconsider and go back down to Georgetown? You could leave your room empty and I could just tell him you're in it. You don't actually have to be here."

Margaret shook her head emphatically. "I shall be protected day and night," she said. She squeezed his arm and kissed him. "By you most of all. And I can't lose so much trade. I am a working girl, you know, and just beginning to develop a clientele here. I can make ever so much more money here than in Georgetown. I only started there to make sure I would work out. They would have brought me here soon even if you hadn't come along. This is where I belong, Skye."

"If you say so. But I wouldn't agree if I thought there could be any danger for you by staying. I want you to know that."

"I do, and I thank you. Jessie was right, you know. You really are a dear man."

"Can't you think of a better way to say it than that?"

She laughed and proved that she could.

Afterward Fargo went back to his hotel to shave and get some much-needed rest. He woke late in the afternoon and wandered down to the livery to check on the Ovaro, no longer concerned about anyone trying to ambush him. Big Dan Finnerty and the unseen employer's toughs had gone back to their usual business, whatever that was. The fact that the chief of police was given complimentary privileges in a whorehouse indicated that not all of that business would be particularly savory.

Fargo saddled the big pinto and spent the rest of the afternoon roaming the country around Central City and enjoying the sights and the crisp, high-country air. He was beginning to adjust to the elevation, at least to some extent, and the Ovaro seemed to mind it not at all.

He spent a lazy afternoon and returned the horse to the livery about dusk. The old man across the street was on his balcony again. On an impulse Fargo went into the boardinghouse—through the front door this time—and invited the old fellow out to have supper with him, Fargo's treat. It wasn't the same as having his own father back again, but it left him with a good feeling nonetheless.

Fargo got the old fellow back to his room early and returned to his hotel. There was no reason he couldn't turn in early himself. All he had to do now was to wait until the false Fitzroy showed up in a few more weeks. And he suspected Margaret would help to keep the waiting time from dragging.

He went to sleep that night with a smile on his face and very few worries. That in itself was a rare treat for the man known as the Trailsman.

Fargo was ambling along the streets of Central City, in such a good humor that he was whistling. He had slept late, eaten well, checked on the Ovaro, and now was on his way to see Margaret. After four days just thinking about her still excited him. Being with her . . . that was even better. His face cracked into a broad grin, and he turned a corner onto the side street that would take him toward Miss Jane's.

As he passed the mouth of an alley he heard a footstep behind him. His mental alarms were sounding even as he whirled, his hand going toward the butt of the Army Colt.

Damn the fat, dumb, and happy inattentiveness that he had been indulging in since he sent that wire.

His mental cursing did nothing to alter the fact, though, that he was trapped fair and square. The hard muzzle of a pistol was prodding into the small of his back, and he had no time to pull his Colt.

He arrested the motion of his hand, and the pressure in his back slacked by a few ounces. The gunman, whoever it was, reached forward to pull the revolver from Fargo's holster and then took him by the shoulder to pull him inside the alley.

There were two of them, Fargo saw now. The one behind him with the gun in the Trailsman's back.

And the man who called himself Fitzroy.

"How in the hell . . . ?" Fargo hadn't expected to see this man for weeks, perhaps for a month or better. Yet here the son of a bitch stood, dressed to the nines and looking almighty pleased with himself.

"I thought you were in New York," Fargo said. He forced a smile he didn't feel and an outward appearance of relaxation. "No matter, I'm glad to see you. I take it you got my wire."

"I did indeed," the false Fitzroy said. "But I have to confess that while I did not mean to deceive you, Mr. Fargo, I was so anxious to see my dear daughter again that I've been keeping track of your progress. From a distance, of course, but not so very far away. I heard you went to Cherry Creek, so I followed you that far. I've been waiting there. As soon as your wire was received at my office, they notified me and I came immediately.''

Fargo shrugged. ''That's fine, but why the guns?''

''My apologies, Mr. Fargo. A man in my position has to take certain precautions against competitors. Sometimes the habit of caution is carried too far. And you are right, of course.'' He nodded past Fargo's shoulder. ''You can put your gun away, Lewis. And return Mr. Fargo's weapon also, if you please.''

Lewis, when Fargo finally got a look at him, was a tall, cadaverously thin man dressed almost as well as the phony Fitzroy. Except that Lewis had a pair of shoulder holsters tucked under the lapels of his suitcoat. His guns were the very latest and most expensive thing in modern firearms, tidily small but quite effective breaktop Smith & Wessons that used the recently patented rimfire cartridges. Cartridge loaded arms were rare indeed out here on the frontier, but Fargo suspected they would become immensely popular once supply had a chance to catch up with the demand that was sure to exist.

Lewis acted less than happy about returning Fargo's Colt, but he did as his boss ordered.

''I believe your wire said that you've not yet approached Margaret?'' Fitzroy prompted. He was relaxed now and very much the hale fellow that he had been in St. Louis. He took Fargo by the elbow and led him back out onto the street, Lewis trailing along behind.

''That's right.'' Fargo glanced over his shoulder toward Lewis, who, he couldn't help but notice, was in a position providing maximum threat and maximum personal safety if any trouble should start. Fargo lowered his voice. ''This is, well, awkward, Mr. Fitzroy. I don't quite know how to put it delicately, but, well, your daughter . . .'' He hemmed and hawed a little, doing some furious thinking as he did so. "You may not want to, uh, become as closely reacquainted with Margaret as you might have thought."

His problem was that Margaret's employer was primed to put a full-time shield of protection around the girl. Round-the-clock bodyguards had already been arranged.

But that protection wouldn't be put into place until the false Fitzroy was expected to reach the mountain town. Not for weeks.

Right now Margaret would be alone in her room, with only the regular bouncer in the house to help protect her. Worse, she was waiting for Fargo to join her. No one at Miss Jane's would think it at all out of the ordinary if Fargo showed up and went to her room, even, probably, with other men accompanying him.

Fargo would have spent some time cursing himself for a fool except that that would have accomplished nothing.

He was becoming seriously concerned now about Margaret's safety.

And the Trailsman had made both her and himself a promise that she would come to no harm from the man who was now walking at Skye Fargo's side.

"I don't understand your inferences, Mr. Fargo," Fitzroy was saying.

"I don't know how to put this any way but bluntly, Mr. Fitzroy. You should understand that it may be painful for you to hear." This was the sort of thing Fargo would be expected to say to the girl's father. He didn't dare let the impostor know that Fargo was aware of the deception; a stranger would be unlikely to give a spit if the girl he wanted killed was or was not a whore.

"Then by all means be blunt, Mr. Fargo. Whatever it is, I have the right to know. And I can asure you, whatever information you have, I'm still most anxious to see my dear Margaret again."

"Yes. Well"—Fargo took a deep breath—"the truth is, Mr. Fitzroy, that Margaret Anne is making her living, well, as a, uh, soiled dove. So to speak."

Fargo was actually fairly pleased with himself. The performance should have been convincing, he thought.

The man who called himself Fitzroy would have made a fair stage actor himself. He gave a creditable performance of shock and grief and concern. But in the midst of all that make-believe shock and concern he was able to pull himself together with manful aplomb.

"I see, I see. It is terrible, Mr. Fargo. Shocking, of course. But Margaret is my only child, Mr. Fargo. The child of my flesh. No matter what her past, I intend to make her future a rosier one."

Fargo damn near broke into applause for the performance. "You still want to see her, then?"

"Of course. As quickly as is humanly possible," the phony Fitzroy declared.

This time Fargo believed him. "Then follow me, sir. I'll take you to her right now."

Son of a bitch, Fargo told himself as he walked.

The people he'd been counting on to help ensure Margaret's safety were not ready. As far as they knew, as far as Skye Fargo had known, there was no reason for them to expect Fitzroy so soon. So it looked like the whole thing was going to be up to the Trailsman.

He was acutely aware of the threat of Lewis, who was still hanging a few paces to the rear and just slightly to the side of the path Fargo was taking. That put Fargo at a decided disadvantage when this thing reached the bursting point.

He had little doubt that something was going to blow, and damned soon. This man who called himself Fitzroy almost had to be behind the attacks on Margaret Anne. Certainly no one else had expressed any interest in the girl.

The belief that Fitzroy had lied to him, had used him, fueled Fargo's determination to block the man's efforts, whatever they were. Dammit, he had played Skye Fargo like a piano, played on his deep concern for the sanctity of the family, played on Fargo's own past to force the Trailsman into a job that was itself nothing but a hollow lie and a deceit.

That was unforgivable, and Fargo intended to have it out with Fitzroy. But first he had to pull the man's teeth—meaning Lewis—and ensure Margaret Anne's safety.

Then, by damn, Fargo figured to have some straight answers from this man who was not the sad and repentant father of a missing girl.

He took them toward the whorehouse by way of the busiest of the business streets of Central City, hoping that by some happy coincidence one of Big Dan Finnerty's less stupid officers—if the venal police chief had any officers who made it all the way up to a level of average intelligence—might see them and reach the conclusion that something was wrong.

That was an awfully faint hope, though. Neither the police nor the toughs who worked for Margaret's employer had an interest in Fargo any longer. They wouldn't likely become suspicious just because he was walking the streets of the town with two men unknown to anyone locally. Faint hope or not, though, Fargo felt he had to give it a try. Nearly anything would be better than leading Fitzroy to Margaret Anne and stepping politely aside. That would be the same as leading a molester of children to the orphanage.

Fargo tried to come up with a plan while he walked. He could think of nothing. He might have led Fitzroy somewhere else. But where? For what purpose? What he needed, dammit, was a distraction of some sort. He could think of nothing in his limited acquaintance with Central City that would provide him with that.

So he marched boldly on toward Miss Jane's, Fitzroy grimly proceeding at his side and Lewis trailing dangerously behind.

"In here," Fargo said as they reached the short walkway to the front porch of the house.

Fitzroy looked as eager as if he'd been telling the truth about the whole affair. He was trembling with such excitement that his shaking was clearly visible to Fargo. The man turned and gave Lewis a swift glance. Of warning? Of preparation? Fargo couldn't guess what it meant.

Fargo led the way and knocked loudly on the door.

The maid with the nice legs was quick to respond this time. She recognized Fargo and let them in immediately. "Hello, Skye," she said with a smile.

Fargo winced inwardly, hoping it didn't show. During the past several days he had become a familiar figure in the establishment and knew all of the girls on a first-name basis. But he had told the false Fitzroy that he hadn't yet contacted Margaret about her father.

Fitzroy appeared not to have noticed the discrepancy.

The maid gathered the hats from all three visitors and dutifully disappeared with them toward the cloakroom off the foyer.

It was late morning, almost lunchtime and therefore about time for the working girls to be gathering back in the kitchen for their breakfast. None was yet dressed and on duty in the parlor, and no gentlemen guests seemed to be present.

Fargo knew that right now Margaret would be upstairs in her room, waiting for him and for the slow, lazy afternoon of lovemaking they had planned before she would be expected to go on duty for the evening.

But Fitzroy wouldn't know that.

"Wait here," Fargo said. "I'll find out where she is."

Fitzroy seemed about to object, but Fargo was already heading for the kitchen door. Behind him Fitzroy nodded to Lewis and the gunman followed.

Fargo met Miss Jane as the madame was coming out into the parlor. She and Fargo had become friends during the past few days, each of them genuinely concerned about Margaret's welfare.

"Ma'am," Fargo said politely. He hadn't called her anything but Jane since that first night he'd been with Margaret. "I have a couple early customers here for you," he said, giving a slight emphasis to the word "early." He glanced over his shoulder and saw that Lewis was hanging there as usual.

"They'll be wanting to see Miss Jessie," Fargo said. "I know which room is hers, and I'll be wanting to see her too. Be all right if I take them on up?"

Jessie, Fargo knew perfectly well, had been sent down to Georgetown as a more or less permanent replacement for Margaret. He hoped Miss Jane got the message he was trying to send. Including about those "early" visitors.

Miss Jane gave Fargo a perfectly normal smile and nodded pleasantly toward Lewis behind him. "Of course. You can go right up."

Damn, Fargo groaned silently. She hadn't gotten it, after all. No help for that now, though. He thanked her and went back to where Fitzroy was waiting. Lewis was as close behind him as the sound of his own heartbeats, which were beginning to accelerate.

"She's upstairs," Fargo reported.

Fitzroy gave Lewis another dark look of anticipation and appeared to be quite nervous now. "Then hurry, man. I've been waiting so long."

Fargo led the way up the winding stairs. At the top landing he turned, not toward the rear, toward Margaret's large, sumptuous room, but toward the front of the house. Toward the now-empty room Jessie had occupied until she was moved.

The door to the room was closed, as it had been for the past several days. Fargo stopped outside it. "Do you want me to go in first and, uh, try to prepare her?"

"No," Fitzroy said quickly, nervously. He licked his lips and looked at Lewis again.

Fargo stepped out of the way as if making room for Fitzroy to enter ahead of him.

Fitzroy reached for the doorknob, and Lewis' attention was on his boss and on whatever, whoever was behind that door. The gunman's hands crept up toward his lapels. And toward the pair of twin revolvers he carried in his shoulder holsters.

So they intended to kill her on the spot. They didn't want her simply found and identified for them. They intended to shoot her down right here and now and handle the consequences afterward, presumably by swift escape while the place was still in a state of shocked confusion.

Fitzroy hesitated for a moment; then, with a nod intended for Lewis, he snatched the door open and stepped quickly to the side.

Lewis' hands flashed, and as deftly as a magician could have done it the little Smiths were out, leveled, and ready to fire.

Most men, perhaps even the Trailsman if he had been taken by the surprise they believed was theirs, would have been slow to react.

But Fargo was ready.

His hand flashed too, as quickly as Lewis' had done. The big-bore Colt swept up and out.

The difference was that Lewis was aiming at the neatly made-up bed in an empty room. And Skye Fargo was aiming at Lewis' belly.

"Game's over," Fargo said coldly. He had a clean drop on Fitzroy's tame gunman. Lewis was caught out of position and vulnerable. But the damned man refused to believe that it was time to quit.

Incredibly, even with Fargo's .44 Colt cocked and leveled at his gut, Lewis made a try for it.

The man's knees buckled as suddenly as a puppet's with its strings cut, dropping him into a sudden crouch, and even as he dropped, he was swiveling toward the Trailsman, the pair of Smiths swinging away from the empty room and toward Skye Fargo's chest.

And while he turned, Fargo could already see the deadly gunman's fingers begin to tighten against the spur triggers of the lethal little guns.

For half a heartbeat Fargo couldn't believe that Lewis was trying it. But he was. And it was perhaps that selfsame bold audacity that had brought him alive to this point.

Fargo's eyes widened as Lewis' guns sped into position and the lean man's fingers tightened.

The Trailsman fired, his big Colt filling the hallway with thunder and the sour stink of burnt powder.

Lewis' head snapped backward with spine-breaking suddenness, and the gunman's fingers tightened involuntarily, prematurely, his little guns barking a response to the roar of Fargo's Colt, but before the muzzles of the Smiths came on line with their intended target. The pair of bullets went wide of their mark.

And Fargo certainly didn't have to worry about Lewis trying again. Trying anything, ever again.

The lean gunman was just a shade too tall for what he had tried.

When he dropped into that crouch and spun he was counting on being able to duck under Fargo's line of fire. If Fargo had been aiming for his head, even for his chest, it just might possibly have worked. Because the man was almighty fast. Fargo had to grant him that much. He was fast and he had the nerve. What he lacked was the raw luck it would have taken for him to be able to beat the Trailsman. Lewis came up short on that account.

When Lewis dropped into his low crouch, Fargo had been pointing the Colt toward his belly. And even as low as he went, the gunman was just too tall to get under Fargo's line of fire.

The soft lead ball speeding out of the barrel of the Army Colt smashed into the bridge of the man's nose, replacing it with a pulpy red dimple where flesh and cartilage once had been. The ball exited messily from the back of Lewis' skull and sent the instantly lifeless body flying backward to stretch out full-length on the now-stained flooring of the second-floor hall.

"Not quite," Fargo muttered.

He swung the muzzle of the Colt toward the man who called himself Fitzroy, but there was no immediate danger there.

Fitzroy, or whoever he was, slumped against the jamb of the empty room staring down at Lewis' body.

The man was pale. Fargo guessed he was sickened by the gore that Lewis' demise left behind.

There was no point in taking chances on Fitzroy regaining his ability to function, though. Fargo stepped forward and reached under Fitzroy's coat to see if the man was armed.

He found no weapon, but his hand came away wet and smeared with sticky, scarlet blood.

Fitzroy had found at least one of the bullets Lewis lost when the little Smiths fired at the involuntary clenching of Lewis' dying muscles.

There was a rumble of running feet on the stairs behind

Fargo, and the house bouncer heaved into view with a short-barreled shotgun in his hands.

"Put that thing away and help me get this guy into the room," Fargo ordered.

So Miss Jane had gotten the message. It must have taken her a moment to get the bouncer from his basement room and arm him. The man couldn't have gotten upstairs so quickly otherwise.

The bouncer—Fargo thought his name was Ned, although they had had little reason to speak during the past few days—leaned the stubby shotgun against the wall, made a face in the direction of the mess Fargo had left on the floor, and helped Fargo support Fitzroy. Fitzroy's strength was fading, and his knees had begun to sag. There would be worse yet to come as the shock wore off and the pain set in.

With one of Fitzroy's arms over each of their shoulders, Fargo and Ned supported the wounded man and held him upright.

Down toward the staircase Fargo could see an inquisitive head pop into view as Miss Jane came up just far enough to be able to see, and farther down the hall Margaret was peeking out her door. Fargo motioned for the women to join them, and he and Ned carried Fitzroy into Jessie's room and laid him as gently as possible onto the bed.

Ned checked Fitzroy for weapons again while Fargo went to meet Margaret at the door and put an arm around her waist.

"It's going to be all right now," Fargo said. "But you were right that they wanted you dead. The one out there was ready to shoot as soon as the door came open."

Margaret was pale and shaky, but Fargo knew she'd be all right.

"Do you know this man?" He pointed toward the man who had claimed to be her father.

He helped Margaret closer to the bedside and waited while she peered down toward the man who had tried to have her killed. She gave him a long, searching look, then finally shook her head. "I've never seen him before, Skye."

"You're sure of that?"

"Positive."

"Damn."

"He has a wallet here," Ned said. "Got some papers in it. Might tell you who he is." Ned handed over the wallet he had taken from inside Fitzroy's coat, and Fargo opened it.

There was no money in the wallet, although a rich man traveling far from home should have been expected to carry a good deal of cash. Fargo suspected that Ned had already surmised the same thing and taken care of the disposition of Fitzroy's worldly goods.

There were, however, some papers. Two letters and a thin sheaf of engraved calling cards.

All of them, cards and letters alike, bore the same name: Aldus D. Fitzroy.

Fargo looked at them again. The letters in the man's possession were addressed to Aldus Fitzroy, president of some New York firm called A&T Fabrications. The street address was the same one Fargo had been given for contacting Fitzroy.

"Was your father's name Aldus?" Fargo asked.

Margaret shook her head. "No, Daddy's name was Thomas. Thomas Gerald Fitzroy."

"Then who the hell is Aldus Fitzroy?" Fargo asked.

The girl shook her head in bewilderment. Fitzroy stirred and coughed, bringing a froth of red to his lips.

"Who the hell are you?" Fargo asked him.

Fitzroy—for that did appear to be his name—gave Fargo a blank look.

"Look, man, you're probably dying. You've tried to kill this girl. Surely you don't want to go to your death leaving her not even knowing why."

Fitzroy coughed again. A large pink bubble formed at his mouth and burst wetly. The effort of coughing brought pain lines to his forehead. He wiped his mouth weakly, saw the blood there, and looked at Margaret for the first time.

The man's shoulders moved, a slight shrug of acceptance, and he smiled thinly. "I almost made it," he said in a whisper.

"Who are you, man?"

When he spoke again, it was to answer Fargo but his eyes remained fixed on Margaret.

"I'm . . . just who it says . . . there. Al Fitzroy. Brother. Tom was my . . . brother."

"Why in hell, man, would you want to have your own niece murdered?"

Fitzroy smiled again. He was growing quickly weaker, probably losing blood internally. "Tom and I . . . partners in the business . . . long time ago." He paused to rest.

"Yes?"

"Tom . . . patented . . . metallurgy process. Seemed useless. Then. Troubles now. Back East. More manufacturing . . . going to be . . . needed. Tom's process . . . cheaper steel. Valuable. Very. But estate . . . hers . . . Margaret's . . . sole survivor." He smiled grimly. "If I . . . could prove she dead too . . . would have had claim to process. Would have been rich man." His lips twisted, turning the sad smile into one of deep bitterness.

"Rich? Shit, man, I thought you already were rich."

Fitzroy laughed in spite of the pain it cost him. "Rich?

Never . . . quite. Always just . . . a step away . . . hour too late. You know that money I paid you . . . St. Louis?''

Fargo nodded.

''Your own. Had that . . . bitch steal it . . . had to beat her up . . . get her to turn it over . . . after set you up . . . for her.''

Fitzroy gave Fargo a mocking, self-satisfied grin. He died with that expression still on his face.

11

"Are you sure you don't need any help?"

Margaret shook her head. "No, but I thank you for the offer, Skye." She smiled and offered her soft lips for a lingering, bittersweet kiss of good-bye.

The Ovaro was saddled and tied in front of Miss Jane's. Fargo's saddlebags were packed.

"Do you think you'll stay in the East?" he asked her.

She shrugged. "I really don't know. It all depends on what the lawyers there tell me. But don't worry. I have some very influential friends in the legal profession here. They've given me the names of the best men in New York." She smiled. "If Daddy's invention or whatever it is is worth anything, they can handle it for me. If not, well, I can always come back here. Whatever happens, I'll be fine now." Her smile became wider. "Thanks to you, Skye. I'll never forget you."

He grinned. "I think it's safe to say that I won't be forgetting you either, lady. You're kind of special."

She squeezed his arm and laid her head against his chest with a sigh. "You're pretty special yourself."

Fargo looked at her, carving the incredible beauty of those patrician features deep into his memory. A woman like Margaret Anne Fitzroy came along only rarely in one man's lifetime. Never, really, in the lifetime of most men.

The Trailsman should consider himself lucky that his path had led him to this one, however briefly.

"Where will you go now, Skye?"

He shrugged and shook his head. For a moment he stared off toward the crags that surrounded the city. "Somewhere out there," he said, "are the men who destroyed my hope for a family life. I tried to give you what I can never have, and except for the idiocy of that asshole uncle of yours, you might really have been able to find it, or at least something like the love and warmth of your own family. Instead, all I was able to bring you was money. If things work out, anyway. That isn't the same, isn't as good by half. But I reckon it's the best you or I could ever hope for now."

"I hope . . . I hope I'll see you again, Skye. Someday. Somewhere."

"Stranger things have happened, Margaret Anne Fitzroy."

"Nicer things than that couldn't happen, Skye Fargo." She raised herself on tiptoes and kissed him again, briefly this time. It was time for him to go, and they both knew it. To linger here any longer, no matter how sweet the interlude, would do her no favors. His presence now could only hinder her from all the preparations and plans she had to make: for the long, difficult trip east, for all the legal foofaraw that would have to take place once she got there. She had things to think about now that Skye Fargo would be no part of.

He gave her a last peck on the tip of her nose and a pat on her sleek rump, then tossed the saddlebags over his shoulder and went to the patiently waiting pinto.

He was whistling as he walked.

It was a hell of a nice day in Central City, and likely it would be just as nice down at Georgetown.

Hell, he had to pass that way anyhow. And it wouldn't be a bad place to stop. Make it an easy day for the Ovaro. After all, the horse hadn't gotten all that much exercise lately. It wouldn't be wise to push him hard after the long layoff. And at such a high altitude.

Besides, Jessie was down there at Georgetown. Stopping in and seeing her again would be only the decent thing to do as long as he was going right by anyway.

He swung into his saddle and reined the pinto away from the house, thinking about Jessie now so that he forgot to look back and wave to Margaret Anne.

He guided the Ovaro through the streets of Central City and onto the trail.

It was a trail that led inexorably toward . . . fate.

LOOKING FORWARD!

**The following is the opening
section from the next novel in the exciting
Trailsman series from Signet:**

**The Trailsman #61
BULLET CARAVAN**

---

*The Nevada Territory, 1860,
east of the Shoshoni Mountains,
where most trails led to an
arrowhead tombstone . . .*

He snapped awake and lay very still.
He listened, hardly drawing a breath.
The sounds came again.
Soft sounds, dry grass rustling.
Leaves being brushed back.
Loose dirt being moved.
Susurrant sounds.

They would not have wakened most men. But he was not most men. He was the Trailsman, and his senses were those of the wild creatures, his hearing that of a mountain cat, his eyes able to rival the red-tailed hawk's. As he listened, the sounds came once again. Something moved through the little glen where he'd bedded down for the night. No deer, he grunted silently, the pauses not those of a deer. No badger or marten: low enough to the ground, but they couldn't help scurrying even when they prowled. No white-footed deer mice: they'd disturb only grass and he heard leaves being brushed. And certainly no bear: you could smell bear a hundred feet away.

Slowly, the big man raised himself up on one elbow and peered through the night, his lake-blue eyes narrowed. The thick overhanging branches let only a thin filter of moonlight in, but he found the shape crawling through the underbrush to his right. He remained motionless as he saw a fedora pulled low, dark clothes, a face hidden from view. The figure halted, turned on its belly, and started to crawl toward the Ovaro. The magnificent black-and-white horse was tethered but a few yards away, and Skye Fargo shifted his weight as the figure halted only a few feet from the horse, paused, pushed itself to hands and knees. It rose, and he saw a slender man step toward the horse. Fargo waited a moment longer until the dark shape, reached the Ovaro and started to pull the big Sharps Carbine from the long rifle holster hung from the saddle.

"That's enough," Fargo snapped out as he leapt to his feet, the big Colt in his hand. The figure froze in surprise, the rifle half-pulled from its holster. "Let go," Fargo ordered, and the figure remained motionless, hands still on the butt of the rifle. Fargo fired a single shot aimed to graze the top of the fedora, and he saw it snap off a piece of thin branch that almost rested on the hat.

The figure let go of the rifle, dropped low, and dived sideways into the brush. Fargo holstered the Colt as he darted forward, saw the man roll in the brush, come up on his feet, and run. Fargo increased the stride of his long legs as he saw the man was quick, racing through the trees with sharp, darting motions. Fargo dug heels into the soft forest floor and closed the distance quickly. The would-be thief threw a quick glance over his shoulder, saw the big shape on his heels, and darted to his left, swerved to the right, then left again.

Fargo refused to waste time and plunged forward until he was almost abreast of the man. He spun then, reached out with a long, sweeping motion, but the man was quick, ducked low, and twisted away to race forward again. "Damn," Fargo muttered as he followed.

The smallish figure ran straight and dodged between saplings, but Fargo's long legs caught up in a half-dozen driving strides. He saw the figure glance back again, but he was ready, his body tensed, as the man tried to swerve once more. Fargo dived, met the swerving movement with a flying tackle, and went down with his arms wrapped around the man's legs. He hit the ground with his quarry, saw the fedora fall off and a shock of short-cropped, blondish hair tumble loose. The form in his arms twisted free as he frowned, relaxed his grip, and pulled away just in time to avoid raking nails aimed at his face.

"Goddamn, a girl," Fargo muttered, cursed again as he rolled away to avoid the kick aimed at his face.

As the boot grazed his head, he reached out, wrapped one arm around her leg, and yanked. She came down hard on her rear with a yelp that combined anger and pain. He leapt to his feet and saw her turn, try to get up speed to race away again. He reached out with both hands, caught her by the shoulders, lifted and spun, and slammed her back against a tree trunk hard enough to make the breath come out of her with a whooshing sound.

"That's enough, dammit," Fargo snapped, and she stood plastered against the tree trunk, trying to get her breath back.

He peered at a face covered with mud and grime, the

short blond hair matted, mud-caked leaves plastered through much of it, shirt and Levi's torn and covered with dirt. She glared back at him from under the caked grime on her face.

"Why were you trying to steal my rifle?" he asked.

"To blow your goddamn head off," she flung back.

"Why?"

"You know damn well why," she spit at him.

"You're certainly a hell of an unwashed little thing," Fargo said. "Why'd you want to blow my head off?"

"You know that, too, damn you," she snapped.

"I don't know what you're talking about," Fargo said.

"The hell you don't," she glowered.

"I don't. You've got something all wrong. Who are you?" Fargo asked.

"Don't put on an act with me. It won't work."

"No act. All I know is you look like you've been under a rock for a week," Fargo said.

"Two days, and you know it," she said, her voice rising angrily. "Two days of hiding from you bastards in mud and sinkholes, caves and rotted logs."

"Not from me, honey," Fargo said. "You look as though you could stand something to eat." She didn't answer and he reached out, took her arm, and pulled her from the tree. "Come on," he said, and she followed grudgingly.

She cast a wary eye on him as she walked beside him, and he saw a small, upturned nose, mostly covered with dirt, a square face, and a strong jaw. She could be real cute under all that caked-on grime, he mused.

"You've a name," he said.

She didn't answer for a moment. "Betsy," she said finally. "Betsy Cobb."

"All right, now, Betsy," he said as he reached the little

glen and the Ovaro. "Start telling me what this is all about."

She shot a sideways glance at him. "You're really not one of them?" she asked.

"I'm not one of anybody," Fargo said. "Now, I'll get you some beef jerky and we can sit down and talk."

"Talk about what I know about Uncle Zeb?" she asked as she slid to the ground near a birch.

"Whatever you want to tell me." Fargo fished the jerky from his saddlebag.

"Why not?" She shrugged, suddenly agreeable as she sat on the ground and looked up at him.

He turned, squatted down in front of her, and began to take the jerky out of its oilskin wrapper. He was using both hands to unwrap the food when, out of the corner of his eye, he saw her arm come up from behind in a short, sharp arc. He tried to twist away from the rock in her hand, but it crashed against his temple and bursts of red and yellow light exploded inside his head. He felt himself falling, shook his head, and glimpsed her standing, watching, and then the curtain of grayness came over him, smothering the flashing bright lights.

He didn't know how long he'd lain unconscious, but he was alone when he woke. He grimaced at the sharp pain in his temple. He sat up, let his eyes focus, and the Ovaro came into view. The long rifle holster was empty, he saw, and he cursed softly. The beef jerky was gone, too, he noted as he pushed himself to his feet.

"Little bitch," he muttered aloud. It was too dark to pick up her trail, but there wasn't a lot left of the night. He shook his head, cleared away the last fuzziness in it, and pulled his bedroll into the thick brush. He lay down and drew a deep breath as the anger simmered inside him. But he lay silent as a log as he listened to the night sounds. She had fled, and only the humming of night insects came to his ears. He let himself catnap as the rest of the night slowly moved toward dawn.

He was in the saddle when the new day came and he picked up her trail easily enough. She'd gone west after she'd slammed the rock into his temple, half-running for a spell, he noted, then finally slowing. The morning sun took to the skies and Fargo saw her footprints wander north, then east, then turn west again. She had moved aimlessly, he saw, and he halted where the grass was tamped down in a small flat circle. She'd stopped there to rest but gone on again. But now her prints were in a straight line and he saw her footsteps had begun to drag across the ground. She was exhausted, and the dawn had come over her by the time she'd reached here. He reined up, slid to the ground, and began to follow on foot.

A flash of blue in the distance caught his eyes, morning sun glistening on a lake, but her trail turned right and he spied the small cave only a dozen yards ahead, well surrounded by thick brush. She had his big Sharps, he reminded himself as he dropped to his stomach and began to crawl forward. She was scared, angry, and vengeful, and she wouldn't hesitate to use it. The mouth of the cave was small and low, and he paused a dozen feet from it. A line of small, loose pebbles ran across the entranceway.

Fargo cursed inwardly. There was no way to cross over them into the cave without dislodging at least a half-dozen. She'd snap awake and he'd be framed in the entranceway, a perfect target for the big Sharps.

His lips drew back and he crawled sideways to the left side of the cave where a growth of scrub brush afforded ample cover. He slid behind the brush and settled down.

She'd sleep through the morning, he guessed, and he relaxed against the rock outside of the cave.

The sun had just crossed the noon sky when he heard her. He rose on one knee, his gaze on the mouth of the cave. She crawled out, the rifle in one hand, stood up, and looked out across the forest land. She held the rifle casually in one hand as she stepped forward, obviously convinced she'd gotten away safely.

Your second mistake, honey, Fargo thought as he waited a moment longer. She was still caked with dirt and grime, he noted, with a few new layers added. He rose up on the balls of his feet and let her take another few steps forward.

Her back was to him as he catapulted out of the scrub brush. She heard him, tried to turn, but he was on her as she attempted to bring the rifle up. He twisted the gun from her hands and she let out a half-cry, half-curse of pain. Stumbling backward, she tried to kick out and dive for the rifle where it landed on the ground. He stuck his foot out and she tripped, sprawled on the ground, and he was at her in one long stride. Reaching down, he picked her up by the rear of her belt and shirt, lifted her clear of the ground, and carried her to the Ovaro. He flung her facedown across the saddle and heard her gasp of breath. Scooping up the rifle, he swung onto the horse behind her and set the pinto into a gallop. She bounced up and down on her stomach, her little rear rising and falling, and he heard her grunts of pain.

"Damn you," she managed to gasp out. "Stop. I can't breathe."

"Take little breaths," he said as he kept the pinto at a gallop.

"Bastard," she managed between bounces.

The sparkling blue of the lake rose up in front of him

and he headed the horse toward the water: a small, U-shaped lake where narrow-leafed sandbar willows grew to the very edge along with high and thick marsh grass. He rode to the edge of the water, let the pinto go in up to his elbows, and halted. Reaching one arm under her legs, he lifted and flipped the girl off the horse, backing the pinto away as she hit the water with a loud splash. He continued backing until the horse was on the soft sand at the edge of the lake. In the water, Betsy sank, surfaced, flailed her arms, and he saw the mud and grime washing from her.

"Get it all off," he yelled, and she tossed him a glare as she dived again, went underwater, and came up shaking her head, this time with her face clean and her short, blond hair free of matted leaves.

He'd guessed right. She was indeed cute, with a small pug nose, the hint of freckles, and flashing blue eyes that still glared at him. She treaded water as she called to him. "I knew you were one of them, you bastard."

"You were wrong before. You're still wrong," he said.

"Hell I am," she said, and turned in the water and struck out across the lake, her arms moving with short, vigorous strokes. He stayed in place and watched her swim and saw that she started to move toward the shore when she was halfway across the small lake. He climbed onto the Ovaro and trotted around the edge of the water and was waiting on the bank as she neared it. She halted, a dozen yards out, dived, and came up swimming hard in the opposite direction. Her watery path took her across the narrower part of the lake, and he waited, watched, and when she drew close to the shore, he sent the Ovaro around the lake and once again waited by the bank as she neared it.

She stopped, treaded water, and he saw the tiredness in

her face. But she turned again, struck out along the length of the lake. Her strokes were slow now, but she maintained a steady movement, and when she started to edge close to the shoreline, he sent the Ovaro forward again. He was waiting in front of her as she rose in the water, her arms hanging. She walked forward, stumbled, fell, lay half in the water for a moment, and rose again. With weary steps, she clambered out onto the bank and sank down to her knees.

"Had enough swimming?" Fargo inquired.

She glared at him, tiredness in her face. The wet clothes clung to her as a wet leaf clings to a log, outlining full, high, very round breasts where tiny points pushed into the fabric. The bottom of her shirt pressed against a short waist, and the soaked Levi's were tight against full thighs that curved smoothly to her knees. She had a tight, curvaceous little body that somehow seemed to fit the pert pugnaciousness of her face.

"Bastard," she managed to get out between deep drafts of breath.

"You are a hard-nosed little package," Fargo said not entirely without admiration.

She glowered at him as she still fought for breath and the very round, high breasts pushed the shirt smooth. "Why'd you come chasing all the way up here after me if you're not one of them?" she accused.

"Two reasons," Fargo answered. "One, to get my Sharps back, and two, to fan your little ass for clouting me with that rock."

She pushed herself to her feet and started to back into the water again. "You've got your damn rifle. You'll have to swim for the other," she said.

"Simmer down, dammit," Fargo said. "You're not as

hard as you make out." She frowned in instant protest. "You had the chance to blow my head off after you clobbered me with the rock. You didn't take it. I figure we're even."

"How's that?" she snapped.

"I could've put a bullet into you a half-dozen times just now if I'd a mind to," he said, and she glowered as his words speared at her. "Whoever you've been running from, I'm not one of them," he said.

"Who are you?" she asked, suspicion still hard in her voice.

"Name's Fargo, Skye Fargo. Some call me the Trailsman," he answered.

"Trailsman," she grunted. "That's why you found me so easy."

"You owe me some answers for all my trouble," Fargo said.

Her pert face regarded him with a long glance. "I'll give you answers if you promise to help me," she said.

"You get only one promise, honey," Fargo growled.

"What's that?"

"I'll listen," he said.

She frowned as she considered his reply, let her lips tighten in displeasure. "Can I get out of these wet clothes first?" she asked.

"My pleasure, honey," Fargo said.

She half-turned and walked behind a thicket of giant bur reeds that almost hid her from view. He glimpsed flashes of her as she peeled off clothes and laid the shirt and the Levi's over the tops of the reeds where the sun could dry them. A pair of pink bloomers followed, and he heard her voice as she settled down behind the giant reeds. "You listening?" she asked belligerently.

Excerpt from BULLET CARAVAN

"I like to see a person's eyes when I talk to them,"
Fargo said. He waited, and her head appeared over the
tops of the thicket of reeds and he could see broad, beautifully rounded shoulders. "Talk."

⊘ SIGNET WESTERNS BY JON SHARPE   (0451)

RIDE THE WILD TRAIL

Prices slightly higher in Canada
